Seven Shots

Brianna Johnson

PUBLISHING

Acknowledgements

Allow me to say thank you to my fans. You are still with me and holding on strong. Growing as an author has been the best experience of my life, all because of you. Each book I write, I write for you. My only wish is that you allow my books to take you places, even if only for a brief time. Thank you all so much for sticking with me and supporting me so much.

Also, a big thank you to Saija Butters who is an artist with Arbitrary Art. Not only is she an artist but she is my best friend. Some may laugh but she is also my children's step mother. Yes, I know it sounds crazy, but I honestly wouldn't have it any other way. She is my biggest critic, motivation, and guidance when needed most. Without her, my life would be dull but most important my books would be lacking. We grow each other in this art world and I'm grateful to have her by my side. Thank you Saija for just being you.

A big thank you to my new-found friend Jennifer Yatzeck. As an avid reader, Jennifer was able to give me a point of view of my books that most missed. I am forever grateful for her opinion and for being my beta reader. Our friendship will grow, and I am happy to have another friend found by my writing. Thank you, Jennifer, for all you have done.

Last but never least, thank you to my children. Though writing around you has become impossible, I am so glad to have each of you close by. You have given me life and a light of joy that I never knew I would have. Through writing I can only hope you will one day cherish my words. Thank you, Eli, Shyann, and Alana, for just being you. I love you each very much.

Seven Shots

Brianna Johnson

CHAPTER ONE

Sweat is running down my spine and my eyes are blurry. The sun isn't high in the sky anymore so I know darkness will follow soon. Every part of my body is screaming. The scratches on my legs are burning and I know more than likely my ankle is sprained. There is a burning sensation running through my back down to my toes, from the beating I had taken. Splinters cover my body and thorns are sticking out of my skin, but I know if I don't keep running, they will find me. Through gritted teeth I push on; refusing to look back.

The trees and the tall grass are thick around me and the earth below my feet is soft and almost wet feeling. Every few steps I take, my feet give out from under me due to the roots stabbing me. Spider webs come out from nowhere at all times and bee stings are becoming a new normal. With a slight wind to my back I keep pushing forward.

A faint noise suddenly catches my attention. I calm my breathing and pace myself to a slow jog to see what it is. It takes a few seconds for my heart to stop thumping in my brain but finally, I get my body under control and I can hear water running in the distance. It is coming from a direction that I hadn't taken yet, and I can't help but wonder if it is a good idea to even attempt the move. My mind is playing tricks on me from being exhausted and my throat is all of a sudden dry. My thought moves on to being able to wash my naked and wounded body; I make a turn and head for the water. It is a risk I decide to take because at that moment I would either die from dehydration or a bullet.

One thing I learned after three days of running was to use my senses; my sense of smell, touch, sight, and hearing are on overdrive. I catch a scent that doesn't sit well with me. Without hesitation I stop running and squat down in the tall grass. My eyes take a second to focus, because the sun and sweat are causing sight issues. I can see some movement in the distance. My first instinct is to jump up and run towards the movement, but I force my body to not react to the thought. Off in the distance there is another person running from the hunters. It takes some time, but I can finally focus on their face. It is one of the young boys who had come to the lands that day. In an instant my heart picks up speed as a leaf crunches in the distance. In my heart I know what is coming. A shot rings out with an echo and the boy's body goes limp. I lie down and whisper to myself, "seven".

One week earlier...

The work day was going slow and I was ready to get home. All the animals were fed, and their perspective areas were cleaned. It was hard for me to believe sometimes that I, Blair Saddler, owned a wild life shelter. It took me four years to earn a bachelor's degree in zoology and another five years to get my PHD. When I turned twenty-nine I bought a run-down shelter in Florida and turned it around. Now, almost four years and lots of experience later, I've rescued and released hundreds of wild animals. The main goal was to return the animals to the wild, but in some cases the animal couldn't fend for itself if released. That's where my shelter came in. Over the years I gained four employees and a few new friends.

The love and knowledge I gained throughout

the years still didn't touch my personality. Though I had a heart of gold, I still had an edge. Nothing seemed to keep me from speaking my mind. If I thought it, I said it; without hesitation. Some people called it a gift, but most called it a curse. My parents contributed to my spicy personality. My smart ass mouth was given to me by my mother. Mia, my mother, was all bark and no bite where as my father James, was a lot of bite and no bark. I was grateful for their attributes because it helped to have an "I don't take shit from anyone," attitude a lot of times.

The clock chimed and made me snap back to reality. It was five o'clock and time to close up the shelter. One of my employees would come back to the shelter a few hours later and check on all the animals. Another employee would go open the shelter early and get all the animals fed and ready for the day. It was only June and I'd already housed thirteen animals at the shelter. There was hope that at the end of the month that number would be cut in half from releasing back into the wild. With the door to the shelter locked behind me, I headed home.

The next day was my day off from the shelter and I planned to get my hair done. Hair was never important to me and seemed to be the last thing I took care of on my daily routine. It was long and a chestnut brown color. Cutting my hair never seemed to be a good idea before because I didn't think short hair would look good on me. With my mom being a light skinned black woman and my dad being a tanned skinned white man, I was surprised with the hair I was given. It was never curly, and it didn't look like my dad's or mom's. I wanted a change though so on the drive home I thought about what hair style to get.

It didn't take long for me to arrive at my house because I lived close to the shelter. Owning a shelter meant anything could go wrong at any time and I wanted to make sure I was close if it did. Closing my front door behind me, I reached for my phone that was ringing. The caller ID showed it was my boyfriend Tim calling for the thousandth time. Sliding the phone back down in my pocket I walked to the kitchen. Food was the main thing on my mind at that moment. After looking in the fridge I quickly decided two things, one was to eat an apple and go out to eat, and two was to make a fast trip to the grocery store. The phone in my pocket began to ring again. I pulled it out and answered it.

"Hello..."

I waited for Tim to speak.

"Hi Blair. Are you still upset with me?"

Rolling my eyes, I debated about hanging up the phone.

"What do you need Tim?"

I heard him sigh into the phone.

"I wanted to know if we could go for dinner tonight and talk."

I hated the sound of that, but I was hungry and all the sudden curious.

"Sure, that's fine. Let's go to that new place in town."

Not waiting for a response, I hung up the phone.

Our relationship had been weird from the beginning. It all started when we met at a gym two years ago. After moving to Florida, I wanted to join a local gym. The only one in my area that didn't charge too much was the one Tim worked at. After working out, Tim asked me out. As nice as I could I turned him down, but he was persistent. Eventually I said yes and that's when my life changed. The dates became an everyday thing and my feelings finally grew for him. What made it weird was after two years of being with Tim, I still couldn't tell him that I loved him. Love was a strong word to me and I didn't use it lightly. Of course, I cared about him and had deep feelings for him, I just couldn't say one hundred percent that it was love.

Feeling annoyed was something new with my feelings towards Tim. It wasn't often that he messed up and pissed me off but two days prior he did just that. He was supposed to pick me up from work because my car was in the shop. Two hours later he showed up with a sorry ass excuse and I knew he really just forgot me. He tried to make up for it with flowers the next day. The flowers were great but I felt something was wrong. I really didn't want to go to dinner with him because of it, but I knew eventually I would have to face him and find out what was going on. In my heart I had an idea but shook it off to go get ready.

After slipping on a black form fitting dress and some skull earrings, I headed for the door. Heels were never my thing and probably never would be. Being five feet nine made it hard to wear heels and not feel like a giant. Flats were my best friend and I wouldn't have it any other way.

CHAPTER TWO

When I walked into the restaurant everyone stared at me. I couldn't figure out if it was the dress or the "go to hell" expression I had that attracted their attention. It didn't matter to me either way though. I looked around and found Tim sitting in a corner on his phone; the one thing he could never do without. I sat down at the table and almost wondered if he even noticed I was there. It wasn't until he let out a deep voiced "hi" that I knew he knew I was there. The waiter was over in an instant to get my order. After ordering I looked around at the restaurant, hoping Tim would ditch the phone. Looking at the white marble tables you could tell the place was expensive. The ceilings were high, and the walls were a dark blue. Color changing LED lights were along every seam of the walls. The other lights in the place were dimed but not so much to where it made the place creepy. Once the waiter left our drinks on the table, Tim finally put his phone down and looked up at me.

"You said you wanted to talk to me, so talk," I said as I took a sip of my water.

"You look beautiful tonight," he said even though his eyes were looking everywhere except at me.

I rolled my eyes at him.

"Really? You haven't looked at me. What do you want to talk about Tim?"

Getting to the point was my thing. Nothing bothered me more than someone beating around the bush.

"I want to talk to you, but I don't want to ruin our date Blair."

"Look, I love food too much for anything you say to ruin my meal. Spit it out already Tim, you know I hate when you do this."

He looked into my eyes.

"Okay Blair...I really don't know how to tell

you this…I don't want to be with you anymore."

I was shocked by his words. My heart was hurting at that moment but I mustered up my voice to say, "Okay, why?"

Tim rolled his eyes as if annoyed; the nerve of him.

"Blair just…just…leave it at that okay?"

"You're cheating on me, aren't you?"

His eyes got big and his hands went flying, "Blair don't do this here; we're in a restaurant and people are around."

"I guess I got my answer."

I paused then disgustedly said, "I have a right to be angry."

"Let me at least explain Blair."

He reached over the table in an attempt to grab my hand. I pulled my hand back and in a firm whisper I said, "I ought to punch you in the face."

I sat back in my seat and calmly said, "There isn't anything to explain Tim. Don't worry about ruining the dinner because I'm not moving from this spot. You are going to pay for this dinner and anything else I get while I'm here."

Without saying anything he looked down at the table. The pain in my chest wasn't normal for me and in that second, I realized I did love him. Pushing my pain back down inside me, I decided to make his night a living hell.

With a loud enough voice so people around could hear, I said, "So what's the name of this woman you cheated with?"

He gave me a "go to hell" look and refused to answer me.

"You know I will find out so it's better if you tell me."

The waiter brought our food. I stopped him before he could walk away.

"Sir, can I have a bottle of champagne and make sure it's the best y'all have. We're celebrating tonight."

The waiter smiled. "What's the occasion ma'am?"

I returned the smile and said, "Well in just a

little while, I'm leaving my cheating boyfriend right here and he is picking up the tab tonight."

The waiter's face changed and he walked away quickly without another word.

The rest of the dinner was quiet. I watched Tim as I ate. With his fork in one hand and his other hand under the table, he pushed his food around his plate. Cheating was on top of my list of reasons to leave a man and I hoped he suffered without me. The waiter came back with a bottle of champagne and two glasses. Popping the top, he poured two glasses and set the bottle in an ice bucket. In a hurried motion the waiter left and went to another table. When we were done, Tim sadly paid the bill and we walked out of the restaurant.

"Tim, before I walk away and never see your cheating ass again, at least be a man and tell me who the girl is."

With my arms folded over my chest I waited for an answer. Tim slumped his shoulders, but never said a word. Disgusted that he was a cheater and a coward, I gave up and walked to my car.

I had one place on my mind, to my best friend Alex's house. Alex and I had been best friends since fifth grade. We had our normal fights, but it never lasted longer than a day, so rightfully she was the only person I wanted to confide in at that moment. I drove as fast as I could so I could tell her what happened.

It took everything in me not to start crying in my car. A broken heart wasn't something I was used to and I was still surprised I felt the way I did about Tim. My father's voice broke out into my head, "You never honestly know how you feel or what you have until it's gone Blair. So, always make sure you live everyday as if it's your last and make sure to keep your head up in the tough times." A tear ran down my cheek and I pushed it off my face.

Finally, I made it to Alex's house. The lights were on and her car was in the driveway. Alex had a nice house in a nice subdivision. She wasn't married and didn't have any kids. Her life was simple just like mine was. Dating was a thing of the past for Alex. I'd even tried to push her towards dating with no luck. I got out of the car. Without even thinking anything of it, I opened the door without knocking. It was a normal habit we had developed from being friends so long. A glass clinked, so I knew Alex was in the kitchen.

"Alex! I need to talk to you!" I yelled as I walked into the kitchen where Alex was washing dishes.

She dried her hands on a dish towel and laid it on the counter.

"What's wrong Blair?"

"Tim is cheating on me and just ended things between us."

I sat down on the bar stool in the kitchen.

"Did he say who it was with and why? You want some coffee?"

Turning around, Alex grabbed the coffee pot and poured some water in it. It was normal for her to comfort me. We knew how to cheer each other up when we were low in life.

"No, he wouldn't tell me who it was or why he did it. Hell, I didn't even ask why he did it. I was so focused on finding out who it was. What kind of jackass does that? I mean, he knows how much I hate cheaters and how much I can't stand a liar. He should have just broken things off and then went to sleep with whoever."

I stood up because too many emotions were running through me and sitting down didn't help them. Another tear ran down my face. I brushed it off before Alex could see it.

"I will be right back."

I went to the bathroom before my emotions took over and millions of tears ran down my face. I had to get it together or I would fall apart. Closing the bathroom door behind me, I leaned against the door. I closed my eyes, took in a deep breath, and then let it out. When I opened my eyes I immediately wished I hadn't. There on the sink was a ball cap and a watch. Not just any ball cap and watch, but Tim's ball cap and the watch I got him on his last birthday. My heart started to pick up speed and my mind tried to process what I was seeing. Why were Tim's things at my best friend's house? Could he have come by one day with me and forgot his things? I knew better than that. Tim never came to Alex's house unless it was a holiday. Months had passed since the last holiday and I saw Tim with the watch on a few days earlier. My heart started to ache, and a red flash of anger washed over me. Grabbing the cap and watch, I walked out of the bathroom and back into the kitchen.

Alex had her back to me making two cups of coffee. I waited for her to turn and face me. When she turned to face me I was standing there with the cap in one hand and the watch in the other. Her eyes grew big, and her face filled with fear. She stuttered out an explanation as she started to back up; afraid of what was coming.

"Blair, it's not like you think. Let me explain things to you. Just hear me out. He means nothing to me and it was only one time. Just...Just calm down Blair!"

I closed the distance between us and stood nose to nose with Alex.

"Calm down? How am I supposed to calm down when I find out my best friend slept with my boyfriend? I mean what in the hell were you thinking? I came here to talk to you about it Alex! I came to you and poured my heart out to you! You were my best friend for most of my life Alex! How the fuck could you think this was okay? Are you both so stupid to think I wouldn't have found out?"

Alex was pinned against the counter as I felt my hands start to shake. Anger was building up inside of me and I knew if I didn't leave I would really hurt her.

"You are the lowest person on this earth and you were never my friend. If I ever see you again I'll beat the shit out of you. That goes for calling or texting me too. Forget I ever existed to either of you. You and Tim are perfect for each other. Both of you are nothing but shit on the bottom of my shoes. I don't want to hear anything else you have to say. There is no excuse for the pain you have caused and the friendship you have fucked up."

With one final look, I spit in her face and walked away.

CHAPTER THREE

The rest of my night was quiet and filled with alcohol. It wasn't a normal routine for me to get drunk, but the occasion seemed to call for it. I not only lost a boyfriend, but a best friend all in one night. So many memories ran through my mind. It was always great being with Tim. We bonded the most when we took trips to the beach or would run together.

My mind flashed back to our last anniversary. It was fall and the air was finally getting crisp out. After working late, Tim surprised me by picking me up from work. He drove to the beach and got us a hotel room. We spent that night making love. The next morning we got up before the sun came up and went running along the shore of the beach. Running was a playful competition between us. What really made that day amazing was when the sun finally came up, we stopped in our tracks, sat down, and watched the sun peak above the ocean line. Suddenly the playful competition didn't matter anymore. We never said a word. No words were needed. We just enjoyed each other in that moment. Tears brought me back to my bottle of alcohol.

The next morning when I checked my bank account from my phone, I realized I paid for a plane ticket. I panicked and tried to remember where I even booked the flight to go. Franticly I grabbed my laptop. When I opened it the last website I visited was still on the screen showcasing the ticket I bought to Angle Inlet, Minnesota. I printed out the plane ticket and debated on getting a refund. After way too much thinking I decided to just keep it and take the trip to Minnesota. In my mind there had to be a reason I booked that flight, even if I was drunk.

I scheduled for a friend from another shelter to come every day to make sure everything was going okay while I was gone. Afterwards, I called my shelter and Olivia answered. She told me that no new animals had been brought in and everything was running smoothly. That brought me peace as I told her to let everyone know I was going to take a sudden vacation and would be gone for a little over a week.

After spending most of my day researching what was in Minnesota, I finally packed my bags. Since my plane left out early the next morning I wanted to make sure I had everything ready. The weather in Minnesota wasn't anything to be worried about in June. It was scheduled to rain a few of the days I was going to be there and the rest of the days it was going to be warm. I also found out that Angle Inlet was isolated which I figured was one of the reasons I must had decided on it while I was drunk. There wasn't a town for miles from any of the homes. The cabin I rented was the closest to town at forty miles away; which was fine with me. After finding out about Tim and Alex's rendezvous, solitude was what I needed.

Later that night I set my alarm and finally laid down. I had to be at the airport by no later than six for my eight o'clock flight. That would put me in Minnesota by ten. Something in me felt uneasy but I couldn't put my finger on it. Second guessing myself was normal so I figured it was just nerves from being gone from home so long. Pushing my feelings to the side I drifted off to sleep.

****

The flight to Minnesota wasn't bad and I even enjoyed the feeling of "running away" for a while. However, getting off my flight was a different story. Three wrong turns and a whole lot of miles later, I finally reached my cabin. I looked at the map I got from the car rental company, for the local town. After having a hard time finding my cabin, I worried I would get lost trying to find it. I let out a sigh, shoved the map in my purse, I got out of the car, and headed to the door of the cabin.

It was the quietest place I had been in a very long time. A few birds were chirping and there was a slight breeze hitting my face. Home felt so far away but I was okay with it. The owner of the cabin told me where he left the key and that he would be by in the morning to collect my payment. Collecting the key from the post on the porch, I opened the front door.

The cabin was small and cozy. The living room was simply decorated with a couch, coffee table, recliner, and television. The windows had white curtains over them and a dark brown rug was in the middle of the floor. There was no art work or wall decor on any of the walls. From the living room I moved to the kitchen. The kitchen was small with a stove, fridge, microwave, and a coffee pot nestled in the corner of one of the counter tops.

Just past the kitchen was a small hall with two doors on each side of the hallway. I peeked inside of the door on the right. It housed a bedroom that wasn't big but had big furniture in it. The bed was every bit of a king size and there was only one nightstand with a small lamp on it. The curtains were a bright blue and were dancing with the breeze from an open window. On the wall across from the bed a television hung by a metal rod.

Closing the door, I turned and opened the other door. Inside was a bathroom that took my breath away. In front of me was a double sink with a white marble counter top. The tub was in the shape of a big oval. It had at least ten jets in it and a window right above the tub. I got excited because I couldn't wait to test the tub out. In a corner was a stand-up shower that wasn't really anything too fancy. There was a sliding door on the opposite wall in the bathroom. It had a white curtain that flowed to the floor over it. I moved the curtain, slid the door open, and walked out to a porch.

The view blew me away. It was miles and miles of fields with no one in sight. The air smelled sweet with a small hint of onion grass; my new favorite smell. Closing the sliding door behind me, I went back inside. A rumbling noise from my stomach caught my attention. Food was the last thing on my mind, but it seemed like my stomach had other ideas. That only meant that a trip to town was going to have to happen whether I wanted it to or not. I wrapped up my exploration and made my way to my rental.

****

With my map in one hand and the other on the steering wheel, I finally found the little town. It took about forty-five minutes to get there. Besides a small diner there was only a pharmacy, gas station, a dollar store, and police station. Still taking in the sights I pulled into the parking lot of the diner. Parking was easy because the lot was completely empty all the way down the street. I couldn't help but feel like I was in a deserted town. Calling it a small town just didn't feel small enough.

I walked to the diner to get some food. Dining in wasn't an option for me. Even though the town looked empty I still didn't want to be around anyone. Deciding on a burger and chips, I sat down and waited for the cook to finish my order. The waitress was nice and she even gave me a slice of pie on the house. I knew it was because no one would be in to eat any of it before it expired, but didn't care too much because I was hungry. Ten minutes later my food was done, and I was back in my car heading for the cabin. On my drive back I decided that I was going to take a nap after I ate. Then when I woke up I would go for an evening jog to clear my mind. Time away from everyone started to seem more and more like the best idea I ever had. Drunk or not I made a good choice.

CHAPTER FOUR

The air was cool when it hit my body. The weather was muggy, but the wind evened it out. The sky was filled with white clouds and the sun was hot on my back. Nothing was better than running to me. It was the only way I knew to get out my frustration. There was always something great about my body being filled with adrenaline as my feet hit the ground. Some people called me an adrenaline junkie. I didn't care if it was skydiving, white water rafting, or hiking; pretty much anything outdoors was my thing. In my mind it wasn't about adrenaline, it was about clearing my mind. I felt free when I was out in nature.

The map I had, gave me the choice of three trails. Each one equaled out to be about five miles round trip and I planned to travel them all. Five miles was about what I ran everyday so I knew I could do it. The path I took was flat. With the gravel under my feet I kept my head up and breathing under control. The area was breathtaking. There were miles of dirt roads with no cars in sight. On each side of the road I could see tall grass blowing in the wind. Watching the grass dance gave me a calm feeling. The fields were big and had a few trees randomly placed all over. Birds were singing and crickets were chirping loudly. Being there took me back to the country side that I missed at home. It was a feeling I didn't expect to get while I was away from home and definitely since my break up. With an open mind I ran down the road and washed away my thoughts.

Once I got back to my cabin I showered, grabbed a water, and walked out to the back deck. For the first time since leaving home I finally took the time to process what happened. Alex wasn't just my best friend she was like a sister to me. Most of my memories of my past involved Alex and that was what hurt the most. We grew up together, went to the same schools, and when I moved to Florida she moved with me. I built a life and helped her build one too. It hurt so bad to know that someone so close to me could betray me so badly. Alex knew how hard it was for me to trust anyone and she had to have known I would hate her for what she did.

Then my mind went to Tim, whom I didn't know I loved until he broke my heart. I worried that I was the reason he cheated. Maybe I did something wrong? Should I have told him I loved him? Was I not good enough for him anymore? The wind whipped in and blew my hair over my face. Chills ran down my spine and I took that as a sign. It wasn't my fault that Tim cheated, it was his. In the long run he would suffer, and I would thrive from a lesson learned. They were perfect for each other and I was going to be just fine. Turning around I walked back inside and headed for bed. I wanted to get some sleep and decided not to worry about my past anymore while I was there.

That night surprisingly I slept good and even managed to sleep in the next morning. That was something I wasn't used to doing. After getting dressed for the day, I decided to drive into town. It was a little weird, but I almost hoped I would see people in town. Driving down the road that led to town, I saw a man running on the side of the road. Immediately I thought he was just another runner like me but when I got closer to him I wasn't so sure. Mud covered him from head to toe, and he never looked in my direction. After getting a safe distance in front of him I stopped my car. Using my mirrors, I looked back to get a good look at his face. Everything inside of me screamed for me to keep driving. It was rare for me to not listen to my gut, but my curiosity was getting to me. With him running towards my car I scrunched my eyes to get a better look at his face. It was as if he was lost in his own mind. No life was shining in his eyes and he ran as if trying to get away from something. I put my car in drive and raced down the road to town.

The whole trip through town and at the dollar store, I couldn't get the man off my mind. Even on the way back to the cabin I drove slowly in hopes I would see him again. Once I got back, I made me some food and set the rest in the fridge for later. It was hard to eat with the man still on my mind.

Eventually I pushed through my day and went out for my run. The trail I took was a little harder, but I made it back to the cabin all the same. In my mind I was fighting a battle of boredom so I decided the next day I would add in some excitement. On the map was a fourth trail. It wasn't on any road and it was even marked out of my map. It would take a lot more out of me then normally because it looked to be around a seven-mile round trip. The decision was easily made because energy wouldn't be a problem. With all the energy I had stored over the past two days that run would do me some good. Bedtime came early that night with high hopes of an adventurous day the next morning.

I got up early and ate a high in protein breakfast of eggs with tuna. With my water in hand I headed out the door. It was still dark outside, but I could see the sun peeking up over the field line. Getting my stretches out of the way I started out in the direction the map showed me. The wind was quiet that morning and it was really sticky outside. Just from stretching I was already sweating. Once I got close to the trail I began to understand why the trail was marked off the map. It was the largest patch of trees I had seen since being there.

With my heart pumping and sweat rolling down my back I pushed on down the trail. It felt good to have some rough terrain to run on, but I was feeling the burn about halfway through. Making sure to keep my mind off my problems I decided to just soak in the scenes around me. The path stayed dark throughout my run because of the tree cover. The trees were tall and side by side; almost stacked close together. The grass was tall and grew up the trunks of the trees. Moss was growing on the side of a few tress and birds were everywhere. Every so often a flock of birds would jump up to fly and startle me. Without even thinking, each time I would jump. Being jumpy wasn't something I was used to and I didn't know why I was even jumpy. The thought of the muddy man came back to my mind and I regretted it instantly. It sent a cold chill down my spine and a sharp pain in my gut. Off in the distance I could see where the trail ended and had hopes of a quick run back home.

I reached the end of the trail and noticed a piece of paper on the ground. I reached down and picked it up while I attempted to calm my breathing. With the paper in my hand I started to run in place to keep my heart rate up. The paper was blank and not worn so I wondered how it got to where it was. Another cold chill ran down my spine and I knew I needed to get back to the cabin fast. Tossing the paper back on the ground, I started to run back towards the way I came. A slight breeze slapped me in the face and I stopped dead in my tracks. My heart was beating fast and my mind was racing. It took me less than ten seconds to react but unfortunately it was nine seconds too late. Someone came up behind me and slapped a rag over my face. The smell made my head hurt and made me want to throw up. In seconds I was on my knees and losing the light in my eyes. I was passing out and I could only scream in my head. Someone had me and I couldn't fight back.

****

A throbbing pain slammed into my head and my eyes were heavy. There was a faint noise that sounded like talking but I couldn't make it out. Words were trying to form in my mind and the memories of what happened to me faintly fluttered around. Something stuck me, and my eyes flew open. In my mind I was screaming but nothing was coming out of my mouth. The world around me was blurry and the bright light didn't help with my vision. My body was weak and I couldn't move. My legs and arms were strapped down. The room smelled of bleach and my clothes were gone. I was naked with only socks on my feet.

I was startled by a deep voice beside me.

"Ahhh, you are awake," a man with a thick and foreign accent said. My guess was that he was British, but I couldn't be sure.

Words wouldn't come out of my mouth and I began to panic. With my heart beating fast I forced myself to focus on where the voice was coming from. Blinking a few times helped a face come into view. With eyes a bright blue and hair a dark brown, the man stood next to me looking down on me with a smirk on his face.

My arm was burning so I looked down to see why. Another man was sitting in a chair next to me. A needle was moving in and out of my arm and blood was dripping out. I watched him closely as he took the plunger off and put a new one on with a small black part inside it. *Is that a fucking tracking device?* I could talk in my mind, but words still refused to come out of my mouth. Looking back at the other man standing over me, I did my best to give him a "go to hell" look. It must have worked because he gave me an evil smile.

"I am sure you are wondering what's going on. Allow me to help you a little bit sweetie. You are a prize that I just had to have. You are on my land and I plan to use you wisely. This gentleman here is putting a tracking device in your arm, so don't try to escape."

I gave him a confused look. *What does he mean he had to have me and where is his land at? More importantly was what did he mean by using me wisely?*

"Let me back up just a little bit for you, I sometimes forget that they drug y'all pretty good. So, I have been watching you for a few days and while doing so I realized that I had to have you. That's why my friend here grabbed you while you were out for your run. You were brought here just a few hours ago and put in this chair. You can't talk but don't worry that will come back soon. It's just a side effect of the drugs we give you. Listen and listen good sweetie. The rules are simple on my lands and I will have someone explain them to you soon. The main thing is that you remember your number and do as I say. Your name does not matter here. You have a number just like everyone else. You are to answer when your number is called. Oh don't worry; this gentleman here will make sure you remember your number."

With that he walked away.

I watched the other man put away the needle and walk to the edge of the room. The room was all white and a small table set in the corner of the room. For the first time in a long time I was scared. The smell of something burning brought my attention back to the man. He had a metal rod and was walking towards me. Fear ran through my body and for the first time I was able to move. It didn't do much good to move with my body strapped down, but I still had to try to get away. At the end of the rod was a red-hot set of numbers and I knew that they were going to brand me like cattle. He gave me a frown and looked down at my legs.

He looked me in the eyes and said, "I am sorry for this, but if I don't do this then I will be punished."

In one swift motion he pushed the hot rod on my leg. Finally, my mind allowed my mouth to speak and a loud scream came out. A burning ran through my legs up to my groin. The pain was unbearable. Without control, my teeth clamped together and my body started to shake. The smell of burning flesh hit my nose and I almost vomited. The man took the rod off me and walked back to the table in the corner.

In a quiet voice I mustered out a whispered, "Please help me."

He walked back towards me with a rag and before I could speak again he placed the rag over my face. Darkness once again hit me and my mind gave up the fight.

CHAPTER FIVE

When I woke up I was naked and encaged. The cage was big enough for me to sit up in, but that was about it. I couldn't stretch out my legs and there was nothing under me to keep me from touching the ground. There was a bowl in my cage and a hamster bottle with water in it on the drab metal cage. A nearby cough made me jump. I turned around to face the noise and my mouth dropped open. All around me were other cages like mine with other people in them. They were all naked, dirty, and muddy. Some were men, some were women, and some were children that couldn't have been more than fifteen or sixteen. They were people of all races and ethnicities.

The man who coughed, coughed again.

With a quiet voice I tried to talk to him, "What is this place and what are they going to do with us?"

He gave me a confused look and then started to eat the food in the bowl.

Another man in another cage spoke to me.

"He doesn't speak English. A lot of them don't. We are on the hunters' lands and we are now animals to their sick game."

With my leg burning, I tried to position myself where I could see him better.

"They hunt all of us? How long have you been here?" I felt my voice growing louder as I continued. "Is there any way to escape?"

"You must be quiet because if they hear you talking you will regret it. I have been here for over a week now. There isn't any way to escape and I suggest you don't try it. I did and let's just say it's not worth it. They put tracking devices in us all and even if you outrun them they will find you when your body gives out. Then they will beat you almost to death. Just do as they say and..." he said in almost a whisper, "if you are chosen, run as if your life depends on it."

I was confused. He told me not to run away but to run when released. "You said not to run though."

He shook his head and looked down at his feet. "Only run if they choose you for the hunt. They will explain..."

His sentence was cut short when a tall man came by with a cattle prod and rammed it in his cage. The man then walked over to my cage and rammed it inside of mine. The prod touched my back and I let out a scream. With my body shaking, I tried to move to ease the pain. Unfortunately, when I moved to ease the pain my leg shot a full load of pain through my body. Needless to say, that was the end of our conversation. I sat in my cage and tried to remain calm until someone let me out. It was a twisted thought, but I hoped someone let me out for the hunt because my body couldn't stand being curled up long. Plus, I was determined to find out what was going on and what the hunt was all about. The man may have given up, but I was damned if I would give up. One way or another I was going to get out of the shit hole of a place and I would make damn sure all of the other people escaped too.

****

That night was quiet because no one talked due to fear. I could not sleep due to the aching of my body. At one point, early in the morning, I finally drifted off but was awaken by a loud alarm that sounded like an air horn being blown through a speaker. Shortly after, a firm voice came over the speaker.

"Today's numbers are…1-0-2-4…2-7-6-5…0-4-5-9…"

I prayed I would be picked for the hunt. I was eager to get out of the cage and figure out a way off the land. I waited and looked down at my leg; 2965 was my number. My heart began to beat fast and my mind started to race.

"0-9-8-7…3-2-8-8…2-5-6-7…1-1-8-9…2-0-0-1…2-9-6-5…and 3-0-0-0."

This is it. I can finally figure out what is going on.

"If any of these is your number, put a hand up through the cage and someone will be there to retrieve you."

The fear of if I bit off more than I could chew crept into my mind. With my hand shaking, I put it through the bars and raised it up. It didn't take long before someone rushed over and unlocked my cage. The man reached in and grabbed me by my hair and pulled me out. Anger flooded my mind because I would have gladly gotten out of the cage on my own. He didn't care though; time seemed to be an issue with him. Keeping a hold of my hair the man pulled me to a barn near the cages. Other prisoners were being pulled behind me and I got a glimpse of just what I was getting into. Seven men stood lined up with camouflage overalls on and guns over their shoulders. The man who gave me the evil smile the day before stood in a suit next to them. Once I was close to the men, I was released and told to stand in a line with the others. The man with the evil smile looked into my eyes.

"Well it looks as if we have a new comer entering the hunt today gentlemen. I must play fair and let her know of all the rules."

He carried a clipboard with some papers on it and a pen in his other hand. In somewhat of a swift motion he walked my way. Once in front of me he spoke in a loud voice for the others to hear.

"My name is Rich, but you will all call me Boss. The rules are very simple here on the hunting lands. There are seven hunters and ten animals. In case you haven't figured it out, YOU are the animals. Here on the hunting lands you will do all you can to survive. Each hunter is only given one bullet and each animal is given a twenty minute head start. You will be set free to run on the hunting lands, but be careful because these seven hunters will be trying to find you. The hunt can last as long or as short as it takes, but remember it takes seven dead animals before the hunt is over. Only three of you will return alive. Once the seventh shot has rang out you will be picked up and brought back here. If you make it today, you are automatically put into the hunt tomorrow. If you manage to survive three hunts, then you are given something special. Not many have made it, but that's part of the challenge."

The man winked at me and walked back to the end of the line.

"Now does anyone have any questions for me?"

He waited for a minute for someone to say something, but no one said anything. The man looked at each person and in a creepy deep voice said, "RUN".

In an instant everyone took off running in all directions. I forced my feet to move and ran as fast as I could. All I could think about was him saying twenty minutes. My goal was to put as much distance as I could between me and the hunters. Gratefulness washed over me because I was happy to be out of the cage, but also because I was used to running. That was one thing I had going for me. I controlled my breathing as I ran, taking turns left and right as I saw fit. The ground under my feet was rough and I felt thorns stabbing the bottoms of my feet. Knowing my life was on the line I pushed forward. Sweat started to form around my hair line, but I didn't let it stop me. Never looking back, I picked up my speed. The land was flat but covered with trees and tall grass. It would be perfect coverage if I needed to rest for a few minutes, but I planned to not make that a habit.

A gun shot rang out that made me jump. When I jumped my foot got caught on a tree root and I fell onto the ground. The pain from my leg being branded shot through me but I jumped back up and continued to run.

"One…"

I knew I needed to keep track of the shots; once

I heard seven the day would be done.

Three shots later, I was still running. It felt like I had been running forever, but the sun hadn't moved much higher in the sky. It could have only been two hours or so into the hunt, but four people were dead. It hurt me to think about the others who were dying and/or running for their lives, but I couldn't let that cloud my mind. I had three more shots to go before the hunt was done. My body was on fire and every footstep caused my mind to scream and each scream hurt my head. Just as I decided to rest my body another shot rang out and made me stop in my tracks. It was much closer than the other shots and it scared me. They were catching up to me so I needed to get moving.

Pushing off of a tree next to me, I lunged myself forward. Only two more shots to go and then I would be able to rest. The trees started to spread out and became thinner. It worried me, but I kept going and made sure to make random turns in different directions. Running in a straight line only helped hunters find you. It was something I was told when I saved a lion cub from hunters. They bob and weave to keep from being hit; it amazed me how smart they were. I was the animal now and had to push my way on.

Suddenly I was forced to stop again but this time it wasn't because of a shot. In front of me I had come to the end of the tree line. It would be a death sentence to cross out in the open, but I didn't know what else to do. I crouched down in the tall grass where I was and got my breathing under control. Something wet was under my feet and it gave me and idea. With my hands I scraped the ground and rubbed the muddy soil all over my body. As quiet as I could, I pulled grass up from the root and stuck it to my body with the mud. It was a big risk to do what I was about to do but it was a risk I was willing to make. One way or another I was going to find out just how good the hunters were.

CHAPTER SIX

The field was full of grass that came up to an average person's waist and I planned to use that to my advantage. I made sure I covered my tracks from scraping the ground and pulling up the grass, then I laid on my belly. I army crawled to the middle of the field. With my breathing under control I laid flat on my stomach and didn't move. My hope was they wouldn't come out to the field and if they did they wouldn't be able to see me because of the grass. The plan could backfire, but my hopes were high. If I could make it two more shots, I would be in a win-win situation; my body could finally rest and my plan would work.

Every part of my body hurt and the mud on my open branded wound didn't help. It was not only burning, but also itching like crazy. I knew I had to push the pain out of my mind. It was mind over matter and I had to dig deep to control it because with every thought of pain my body tried to shake. Shaking would draw attention to the grass and I couldn't have that.

A slight noise caused me to hold my breath. I tuned into my hearing and waited for another noise. It took a second, but I finally placed the noise. It was footsteps coming from behind me. In that instant I wanted to run but knew it would be a death sentence if I did. Staying calm, I controlled my breathing and tried to slow my heart rate. It felt like I was in a horror movie and I wished it was all over. Laying my head to the side I closed my eyes slightly. Right next to me was a tall man wearing camouflage with a gun pointed in front of him. Biting my lip, I held back any noise that could slip out and held my breath. My mind tried to drift to the fact I was about to die but I pushed the thought out. Focusing was my number one priority. As if on que the man shot his gun and the loud ring hurt my ears. Luck must have been on my side or I had anticipated the shot because I didn't flinch. The man put the gun on his back and made a laughing noise.

"Thank god I'm not last today," he said to

himself. He turned and walked back in the direction of the tree line.

With only one shot left I hunkered down and waited it out. It was hours later before the seventh shot finally rang out. I was scared to move and even questioned my counting skills. *Did I count seven shots? Could I be wrong?* Replaying all the shots in my head I was able to confirm that I indeed heard seven shots. I sat up and brushed off the grass and mud from my body. I didn't want any of the hunters knowing what I had done just in case I needed to use the idea again later on. All I had to do was get out of the field and wait for them to pick me up.

Crawling on my hands and knees I made my way back to the tree line. It took a while, but I heard an engine running in the distance. Though it was the people to pick me up, I still had an uneasy feeling in my stomach. There were two guys on four-wheelers. The man who branded me pulled up next to me and waited for me to get on. I got on and rode the rest of the way back in silence. Something in me broke in that moment and turned my mind upside down. The events I went through were enough to break anyone and I knew it wouldn't be long before I was completely broken. A plan started to form in my mind and I knew I had to win the prize after three days. That would require me to survive two more full days of being hunted. A new determination washed over my body as I got off the four-wheeler and faced Boss.

"I see you have made it past day one. Tomorrow you will do it again 2-9-6-5. You need to eat and rest."

In an instant I was jerked by my hair and pulled back to the cages. Without thinking I started to fight back. Punching the man in the side and scratching his arm; determined to beat the shit out of him. His grunting let me know I was succeeding and I continued to hit him all that I could. A sharp pain sliced into my side and dropped me to my knees. The man let go of my hair and I rested my body on my knees. Without looking up I knew Boss was in front of me.

"I wouldn't think you'd have much energy left in you after the hunt today, but I see I am wrong. Let me help you get some of that anger out of you bitch. Mitch, take this black bitch to the tress and give her ten lashings. That should help her mind know where it belongs. If that doesn't do the trick, then give her ten more."

He walked away, and the other man pulled my hair again. Dragging me off my feet he pulled me past all the cages. Getting a glimpse of all the cages I noticed there had to be about a hundred of them on the land. Each cage had someone in it that I could see and their face all showed fear. The shelter was run down and looked to be just a metal building that only had one side closed in. The front of the shelter was open and facing the woods where the prisoners were forced to run for their lives. It was an awful place for anyone let alone a hundred.

In that moment I decided I would take the beating for each of them. Being a hero was never on my bucket list, but seeing all the people's faces I knew I had to save them all. No one else was going to do it and I would rather die trying then die from a bullet.

My legs gave out from under me when I reached the two trees in the field. It was far away from the cages and I felt that they were going to beat me within an inch of my life. It was a beating I would have to take because my body was too dead to fight back. Two men pulled my arms and stretched them out by my side touching tree to tree. A rope was placed around each wrist and then wrapped around each tree. Both men cranked on the ropes, so my arms were pulled as far apart as they could go. The pain was unbearable, but I refused to give them the satisfaction of crying out. My head dropped forward, and my knees started to buckle under me.

Whispers were happening behind my back as I embraced the hit that was coming. The first blow jolted my body forward as the swishing sound of a whip slapped me on the back. Pain like I never felt before shot down my spine to my buttocks. It felt as if someone took a razor and slashed my back. Before I could ready myself for another blow it was already there. My body worked against me and jolted forward again. Sweat ran down my spine and into the open cuts. It only made the burning worse on my back. Tears filled my eyes and slowly ran down my face.

A sob made its way out just as another blow hit my back. My mind worked against me and a scream flew out of my mouth when the next blow hit. The man behind me was counting the blows and sounded like he was smiling as he was hitting me. The blows ranged from my back, legs and butt. They wanted to make sure I didn't have any fight left in me when they were done. After the eighth hit to my body the pain started to numb itself and the hits only affected my body. My knees gave out from under me so they pulled on the ropes around my wrist. It forced me to stand and take the beating. With blurry eyes from the tears I started to see things. Visions of my mother's face came and took my mind to another place. I knew it wasn't real, but it was better to think of my mother then of the beating I was being given. Just as fast as the vision of my mother appeared it was gone just as fast. My arms were released, and my body fell to the ground. The only thing I remembered next was waking up to darkness in my cage, with my body shaking from pain.

The man in the cage next to mine spoke to me again.

"You need to eat and drink if you are going to make it on the next hunt. Trust me it's not tasty but it will give you some energy and you will need it more then you know."

I didn't respond to him, but I took his advice. Holding my nose, I ate all the food in the bowl and drank some of the water in the bottle. The food ended up being dog food, but I would take what I was given at that point. Going without food wasn't an option. I put some of the water in my mouth then spit it out into my hand. Trying my best, I lifted my hand and poured the water down my back. It stung but I knew it had to be done. I was damn sure not going to die from infections after dodging bullets and being beaten. Moving to the corner of my cage I propped my body up the best I could and passed out from the pain.

CHAPTER SEVEN

The sound of the alarm woke me again. Pain shot through my body and moving was next to impossible. The first thing I planned to do once I was in line was stretch. I knew it would hurt like hell, but if I didn't there wasn't any way I would be able to run. Boss' voice came over the speaker and a chill ran down my body. I hated his voice and hated his face even more. Once my number was called I raised my hand through the bars and waited to be pulled out. After I was in line and let go, I started to stretch. The hunters watched me with confused looks, but I didn't care. Their eyes all stayed locked in on me and I knew I was putting a bull's eye on my back.

Boss walked to where I was stretching and looked in my eyes.

"Go ahead and work the soreness out sweetie because you are the main hunt today. We want a challenge don't we men?"

He turned and faced the hunters and they erupted in cheers. They knew I was hurt because of the marks on my back and that only put a bigger target on my head. It took a sick person to hunt a human, but it took an even sicker person to find joy in hunting them. Boss explained all the rules again for any of the new comers and once I knew the speech was almost over I stood up straight. It was time to put my pain to the side and run for my life. It wasn't safe to take the same trial as the day before and I decided to take another direction. When Boss yelled "run", I took off like a broken lightning bolt. I ran fast but with an odd limp and that was okay. The key was to be fast and get a good head start. Later I could rest but at that moment running was my main priority.

One advantage I had was four other runners took off in the same direction as me. Once out of the hunter's distance they all split up and took off in other directions. I stayed straight this time and decided to split off later. With my breathing under control I forced my body ahead. The sun was coming up and I wanted it to be on my left side when I turned later. With a good sense of direction I knew where the field was if I needed to use it again. This time I had another idea and was willing to bet I could outsmart the hunters again.

The sun was finally high in the sky and my body was giving out. I decided that it was time to put my plan into action. Only three shots had been fired so part of me worried that it was too soon. It was going to have to work because my body had enough. Slowing down I took in my surroundings and looked up in the tall trees. It took me a little bit, but I was finally able to find the perfect tree. Time wasn't on my side and I had to keep my hearing in check because at any time a hunter could show up.

Wrapping my arms around the tree I started to shimmy myself up until I could reach a knot sticking out. My bare skin was rubbing the tree as I climbed, and splinters were embedding themselves into my skin. With all the strength left in my body I pulled myself up and climbed the tree until I was halfway to the top. There was no coverage in the middle of the trees, so my only option was to make it up to the top. I struggled getting the rest of the way up, but I knew if I didn't hurry, I risked someone seeing me. Then all my work would be for nothing.

With all the pain radiating through my body, I was worried I wouldn't be able to make it much further. My body was giving out and the wounds on my back were hot to the touch. The sun had burnt my skin and blisters had started to form on my body. Not allowing my body to rest wasn't an option. I felt a tear run down my cheek. I was fighting a battle of emotions and up until then I was winning. Pushing myself I slid my body up the tree. It was only about ten more feet to the limbs of the tree, but it felt so much further.

Eventually I reached the top and eased my back up against the tree while sitting on a limb. The floor of the forest wasn't visible to me and that was okay. The main focus for me at that moment was not passing out from pain and falling to my death. Another shot rang out and in my mind, I whispered "four". Laying my head against the tree I started to let my mind wonder for the first time in days.

I thought about my mother, Mia, and my father, James. My father and my relationship was never the same after my mother went missing. My father, called me in a panic saying that my mother hadn't come home. After rushing to my parent's home, I ran inside to find my father crying on the couch. He said she went out to the store to get some food for lunch but never returned. The police were called, and they promised after twenty-four hours of her being missing they would investigate. Now four years later, there still wasn't a trace of my mother.

My father eventually told me that my mother might have just run away. The reason behind the possibility is what caused me to lose my relationship with my father. Like most men in the world, his mind wondered from time to time, but it was his actions that got him in trouble. He wasn't faithful to my mother and had told her so the day she went missing. After four years I still couldn't believe my mother would run away. I was her pride and joy, so even if my father was a cheater it still wouldn't have mattered.

It was hard for me to leave home, because I still had faith that my mother might return. However, I feared if I didn't then I would have wasted my life waiting for something I wasn't sure would ever happen. Not long after I moved to Florida to start my new life, my father moved near me in an attempt to patch up our relationship. It of course was a failed attempt. It infuriated me even more because I worried that with us both in Florida, my mother wouldn't have anyone to come back home to. Pain filled my heart at the memories of my mother.

A gun shot went off below me and snapped me back to the present. It worried me that I allowed them to get so close to me and I not have heard them. Pushing memories out of my mind I went back to fight mode. My ears were wide open, and the crunching of footsteps was below me. There was a hunter close to me and I hoped he had already used his bullet.

I dared not move and barely breathed; not caring that I was forty feet up in the air. The slightest movement could send broken bark down the tree or give them a sign of where I was. Determination flowed through my body and I closed my eyes. Nothing was going to move my focus to anything other than the man below me. Someone talking caused my eyes to fly open. There was more than one hunter below me and it caused my heart to pick up speed. They were helping each other hunt. Only one shot rang out close to me so one of them still had a bullet left.

"I got one of the bitches but it's not that smartass one that Rich told us about. She is worth a lot more than the others, so you need to find her Mark. If not today, definitely tomorrow. We can't let her win at any cost."

"I know, but she is hiding very well. Even the tracker hasn't been able to find her," I heard them say before I heard footsteps.

The rest of the day went by slowly. It took longer for all the shots to ring out, but eventually I counted all seven. My body was stiff, and I didn't want to move from the tree limb, but I didn't have a choice. As careful as I could, I shimmied back down the tree in slow motion. Closer to the base of the tree I lost my grip and slid down. The front of my naked body screamed in pain. My chest had scratches all down it and blood started to pour out. Splinters were sticking out of my breast, stomach, and thighs. Some were embedded into my skin and the slightest touch burned.

My body was officially covered in wounds from head to toe. It was a worry I had to save for later because I could hear four-wheelers in the distance. Sitting down against the tree I waited for them to come get me. One four-wheeler showed up with a dead girl on the back, she was a young Asian girl with dark brown hair. Her hair was knotted and she had mud all over her naked body. She had been shot in the head. The sight of her body didn't bother me as bad as her eyes being wide open staring at me. The pain all over my body didn't compare to the pain in my heart. The hunting land was a terrible place and so many people were dying. The man just kept moving past me. He was picking up only the dead bodies and I couldn't stop thinking about that poor girl. I leaned against the tree trunk and waited to be picked up. Later another four-wheeler came by and got me. Just like the last time, Boss was waiting for me when I came back.

"Ahh, I see you have made it another day. You look hideous, but it doesn't matter. Get some rest because tomorrow you will need it. I GUARANTEE it will be a hunt like never before."

He winked at me and turned away swiftly. The blood in my body was boiling and killing him was my number one priority. There just wasn't enough energy in my body to kill him yet.

CHAPTER EIGHT

That night I was fed and given more water. I managed to wash my body off and still had enough to hydrate myself. I had open wounds from the whip beating and the branded mark they gave me, as well as a whole new scar collection from the tree. That didn't count the sunburn and bug bites. It amazed me how much pain I was able to take, but I figured that happened when your life was on the line. It took a while but eventually my mind shut off from the pain and thoughts, and finally I fell asleep. Dreams eventually filled my mind and replaced the nightmare I was living.

The next morning, I didn't want to wake up. Somehow, I managed to sleep all the way through the night without getting up. It surprised me seeing as to how I was in a small cage and in a large amount of pain. Rest was what I needed most and something in me sparked. I had an energy burst flowing inside me that I had not had up until that point. A new sense of urgency ran through me and time was ticking for me to make an escape plan. If I made it through that day, then I would be able to get the prize. It was the light at the end of the tunnel. Something good was waiting for me at the end of the hunt; one way or the other I was going to make it out of the forest alive.

With the same routine in play I lined up with the other people. Before I started stretching, I glanced over at them to see if any of the others had made it from the previous hunts. The only familiar face was a young boy I had seen when being taken to get my beating the first day. My splinters were pushing up and the lashes on my back were screaming as I stretched them out. It felt like I was ripping more skin off my back with every bend I made. Boss walked to where I was stretching and grabbed me by the hair. Anger washed over my body in a whole new way.

"This black bitch here has made it to day three of the hunt. How you idiots have managed to not kill her already is beyond me," he said as he pulled me down the line.

"She is the main goal today gentlemen. I understand that a kill is a kill in your book but please remember the price that is on her head. This is a challenge like never before. I am going to change things up for some fun. What do you say 2-9-6-5?" he asked me smugly as he shoved me on the ground as hard as he could.

Pain rushed through my body but I refused to show him any sign of weakness.

"Today we will give all the others a twenty minute head start but her...she only gets ten minutes. You gentlemen only have twelve hours to hunt today so make it count. If you come back empty handed then you know what happens. With that being said, you need to kill something today even if it isn't her. Just be sure to look very well for her, because I really don't want to have to keep my promise if she wins."

He looked at the others and told them to run while looking at his watch. Time passed slowly and my heart was beating so fast. Ten minutes didn't give me much time for a head start but I didn't have much of a choice. My legs couldn't fail me and my mind had to be sharper than it ever was before because a price was out on my head. Getting to my feet I waited for him to tell me to go. Footsteps sounded behind me and within seconds Boss was behind me. His breath was hot on my neck and his hand was pushing my hair to the side. As soon as I felt his lip slid across my ear I flinched. One word was said that sent me running with chills down my spine.

"Run..."

Run wasn't the word for it, I raced forward and off into the woods. It was dangerous, but I went the same direction as the day before. I wanted to throw them off and decided once I was in the woods I would turn and go in a new direction. The sun was already coming up and just its slight touch on my skin hurt. My sunburn was brutal, and I hoped I had time to stop to throw on some mud. It was the only sunscreen I had in nature. Weaving through the trees, I forced my body forward. The clock was ticking. I had to move and move I did. Jumping over roots and leaping over puddles, I gave it my all. The only thing between me and the prize was seven people and twelve hours. With no idea what the prize was I knew it would be good. Boss talked about it like it was something he would dread giving to me, which meant it was important that I got it. Plans for an escape played through my mind.

It was a struggle to think about it while running, but I had to put some thought into it. In that moment I decided to put it aside until I knew I was a good distance away from the hunters.

As if my body wasn't already hurting enough, I jumped and landed wrong. A root that was sticking up caught my foot on the way down. When it caught my foot, it stopped me and I slammed into the ground. I broke the fall with my wrist. I was glad I did because there was another root sticking up inches from my face. It would have knocked me out and the hunters would have found me for sure. Forcing myself to stand up was another pain I didn't want to experience. It was another wound to add to my list and just another reason to get off the land. I took a few seconds to stretch and rotate my ankle around, then went back to running. It wouldn't be long before I would have to rest. My ankle was hurting badly and running would eventually be impossible. Until that moment came, I bite through the pain and kept running until I couldn't anymore.

The sun was up fully and no shots had rung out yet. At that moment I knew they were only hunting me. If I could make it close to twelve hours they would be forced to hunt the others, because if they returned with nothing, they would have to deal with

Boss. Something good was on the line for them also and I knew they wouldn't risk it. A hill came into view with thick trees on it but no grass. The rain water in the past must have caused the grass to not be able to grow on it. Taking a sharp left I ran up the hill and weaved through the tall thick trees. Going uphill proved to be a struggle like I never imagined. With each step my ankle popped and put strain on my leg muscles. It wasn't broken but I couldn't be sure something wasn't torn or sprained.

Once at the top of the hill, I took a second to rest and looked down on the land below. Being naked and out in the open took a major toll on my body including my eyes. They weren't as strong as they were when I got to the hunting land. The sun didn't help, but one thing that I was sure of was the movement coming in my direction. It was a good distance from me, but it wasn't far enough away for my liking. The slow-motion movements let me know it wasn't another person being hunted. It was the movement of a hunter. Just as my heart started to beat faster my feet took off. I needed to get distance between me and the hunter and I had to do it quickly.

Being quiet was a challenge running through the woods with an injured body. Every step I made was loud. It was something I dealt with because speed was my goal and not being quiet. Trees started to become a blur and I was running faster than I ever had before. My body was on overdrive and I was thankful for it. Adrenaline pumped through my body and it helped push the pain out of my mind. Bushes with thorns on them started to stab my body in every direction. This was a new location for me, but I was grateful for the cover it provided. Some bushes were tall and stood just above my head and others were short around my ankles. It hurt like hell to run through them, but I didn't have much of a choice. As I ran the bushes became thicker and bigger. Before long I was elbow to elbow with thorn bushes. Just as I started to feel safe and that I could slow down, a rushing noise caused me to stop. I searched franticly around for somewhere to hide or something to hide under, but the only thing around me was thorn bushes. One of them had a small round hole in it around the base of the bush.

With my heart beating wildly and my mind running scared; I forced my body inside of the hole of the thorn bush. Thorns were ripping off the bush, embedding into my skin, and blood poured out of my arms, breast, legs, and butt. With each hand I grabbed a branch and pulled my body further inside the bush. The thorns pushed their way into my hands and made them bleed as well. Tears ran down my face and anger filled my blood. I wanted it to all be over and all the pain to stop. One person shouldn't have to endure all that I had. Every emotion a human could feel I had felt it over my days on the hunting land. It was enough to break someone, and I had to get it under control before whatever the noise was, came for me. Suddenly a shot rang out and I feared I had been hit.

I frantically moved my hands over my body looking for blood. Either my body was playing tricks on me or someone else got shot. It was the first shot of the day and I couldn't have been happier to hear it. It was the cruelest thing I had wished for because someone else died, but I could count my life saved once they rang out. As if there was an echo another shot rang out nearby and it sent another chill down my spine. That was two out of the seven I needed to hear. Unfortunately, that meant I would have to stay put because evidently I was surrounded by hunters. Thorns were stabbed me all over my body and I could feel myself shaking. If anyone came near the bush they would know I was there. Fear wasn't a word for what I felt at that moment; it was defeat. I could slowly feel myself giving up. Luckily it didn't take but a few moments to snap my mind off that thought, but it haunted me that the thought was there to begin with.

It took what seemed like hours, but I finally felt safe enough to get out of the bush. The hunt was lasting longer than the two previous ones I was involved in. There was only one shot left and I was determined for it to not be me that got it. I took off and start running again.

Sweat ran down my spine and my eyes were blurry. The sun wasn't high in the sky anymore so I knew darkness would follow soon. Every part of my body screamed. The scratches on my legs burnt and I knew more than likely my ankle was sprained. A burning sensation ran through my back down to my toes, from the beating I had taken. Splinters covered my body and thorns stuck out of my skin, but I knew if I didn't keep running, they would find me. Through gritted teeth I pushed on; refusing to look back. The trees and the tall grass were thick around me and the earth below my feet was soft and almost wet feeling. Every few steps I took, my feet gave out from under me due to the roots stabbing me. Spider webs came out from nowhere at all times and bee stings became a new normal. With a slight wind to my back I kept pushing forward.

A faint noise suddenly caught my attention. I calmed my breathing and paced myself to a jog see what it was. It took a few seconds for my heart to stop thumping in my brain. Finally, I got my body under control and I heard water running in the distance. It came from a direction that I hadn't taken, and I couldn't help but wonder if it was a good idea to even attempt the move. My mind played tricks on me from being exhausted and my throat all of a sudden became dry. My first thought was of being able to wash my naked and wounded body; I turned and headed for the water. It was a risk I was willing to take at that moment. I figured I would either die from dehydration or a bullet.

One thing I learned after three days of running was to use my senses; my sense of smell, touch, sight, and hearing were on overdrive. I caught a scent that didn't sit well with me. Without hesitation I stopped running and squatted down in the tall grass. My eyes took a second to focus, but I could see some movement in the distance. My first instinct was to jump up and run towards the movement, but I forced my body to not react to the thought. Off in the distance there was another person running from the hunters. It took some time, but I finally focused on their face. It was the young boy. A leaf crunched in the distance. In my heart I knew what was coming next. A shot rang out with an echo and the boy's body went limp. I laid down and whispered to myself, "seven".

CHAPTER NINE

I wasn't sure of the feelings that were running through me. Even though I had made it through three full days of brutal beatings and intense injuries from nature, there was still no future for me if I didn't make an escape. Planning and preparation would have to start soon or else I would be right back in the hunt with the hunters back on my heels. I could hear the four-wheelers coming but I had no energy left in my body to even get up. I could only lay there and hope they didn't mistake me for one of the others who were dead. The wind started to blow over my body and the green onion grass was blocking a lot of my senses. I wanted nothing more than to lay there and rest my body. I knew that I wouldn't be able to but wishful thinking in a bad moment brought some hope from the nightmare.

Someone yelling snapped me out of my slim moment of happiness.

"I think she is dead but you better check Jack. I am going to go collect the others I'll be back."

In a flash the four-wheeler sped off and another one came closer to me. With my eyes closed I kept my breathing calm. It wasn't until the man got off the four-wheeler and nudged my body with his shoe, that my eyes finally opened. The man jumped back and then leaned down to where I was laying.

"Alright 2-9-6-5, get up and let's get going. Boss is going to want to see you. How you managed to live is beyond me, but either way I'm not carrying you so get up and get your ass on that four-wheeler."

An annoying feeling ran through my body and out of habit I rolled my eyes. Huffing out a breath I forced my body to move and roll over. After minutes of struggling I was finally able to get my body off the ground and wobbled to the four-wheeler. The jackass man didn't even give me enough time to get set on the four-wheeler good enough before hitting the gas. As if my body was dead and limp, I flew through the air without hesitation and landed on my back. The man stopped the four-wheeler and got back off.

"You have got to be kidding me."

I could hear leaves crunching and smelt the smell of strong cologne. With my limbs lifeless my body was suddenly floating in the air; I realized he was carrying me. My body was completely and utterly exhausted and I had nothing left in me. After getting on the four-wheeler I slumped my body forward and leaned on his back. The speed of the four-wheeler almost knocked me off a few times, but I honestly didn't care. Eventually the four-wheeler stopped. The warm body I was pressed up against moved and my body slammed forward. My head hit the handle bars and the world around me went black. I passed out, but I didn't care. My body was finally resting, and no one could take that from me.

****

Things were different when I finally opened my eyes. I wasn't woken up by any alarms and no annoying voice came over any speakers. There wasn't a cage around me forcing me to get comfortable in a corner. I didn't have dog food in a bowl or a hamster bottle of water. I wasn't naked or sitting on the ground. My body wasn't dirty or covered in blood. I was awaken by the sun shining in my face from a nearby window as I laid in a bed.

The room I was in was small with bright white walls. A red robe was wrapped around my body and bandages covered me from head to toe. Someone took the time to bathe me and doctor my wounds; I felt violated at the thought of that. Sitting up I felt my senses kicking back in. For three days my senses were the only thing I had to get me by and they were still on overdrive. Scents of lavender, fruits, body wash, and flowers filled the air. My body ached, but nowhere near as bad as before. Most of my pain was soreness and a few of my warrior marks were burning. Other than that I felt better than I had in a while. I noticed there was a dresser with a fruit plate on the top. Instantly I didn't care about anything else around me and jumped up to get the peaches, pineapple, strawberries, mangos, and grapes that were on the plate. As I stuffed the fruit in my mouth I couldn't help but moan a little. It was the first real food I had in several days.

A clicking noise turned my attention around quickly. I went into hunt mode and crouched down on the floor like an animal. Fear washed over my body as I locked eyes with Boss, who was sitting in a corner with a pen and paper. Backing up I crouched into the corner and awaited whatever was coming my way.

"Good morning 2-9-6-5. I see you slept well and are enjoying the fruit."

With sharp eyes I gazed at him with a deadly glare. It bothered me that I missed him being there the whole time. I allowed my stomach to overtake my mind and it could have cost me my life. Refusing to speak I stayed in the corner watching his every move.

"It's okay 2-9-6-5. You can sit down on the bed and eat the fruit. I promise to not harm you. I'm just here to talk to you."

He waved his hand towards the bed and stood up. Flinching I watched him walk to the dresser where the fruit was sitting. He picked up the plate and set it on the bed. Afterwards he walked back to the chair and sat down.

"Come on 2-9-6-5. I haven't lied to you yet so why would I start now. If I wanted to harm you then I would have tied you down and not brought you food."

It was hard to understand it, but I knew he was right. I stood up slowly, kept my eyes on him, and walked to the bed. Sitting down I started to eat but never took my eyes off him.

"Now let me do some talking while you eat okay?"

A nod was all I could give him because I was eating so fast. Even if food wasn't there I refused to give him the satisfaction of me talking at all.

"Let me explain why you are here. First, congratulations to you for somehow surviving three full days of being hunted. Now let's get to the prize, shall we?"

Sharp fear ran down my spine. I felt as if something was wrong.

"So, when you are able to survive three days of a hunt you win two nights here. You are fed three times both days and given full luxury. You will get to sleep in a bed, shower, see a doctor, be given clothes, and are able to walk the lands at your will; with supervision of course. Also, you will be given four options of an item to take with you once you return to the hunt. We will get to them later, but for now this is your first day here and you should enjoy it."

"What's the catch?"

I heard him suck in a breath as if to debate on telling me something.

"That's the thing, there isn't any catch. I do this for all my animals that come to the lands. I choose them carefully, but very few make it as far as you have."

Questions flew into my mind.

"Why did you choose me?"

Putting his pen down he looked in my eyes.

"You…you were chosen because of someone else. You are here because someone here talked about you and made me have to have you."

Confusion ran through my body.

"You weren't a random choice and I can see you are confused. You honestly thought you are here because I chose you at random?"

I pushed the food away from me and waited for

him to continue.

"Blair, I followed you for many months. It wasn't until you were faced with your break up and the realities of your slutty friend that I knew it was the perfect time to strike. I had to be careful when I took you. I almost gave up with getting you, but my precision and planning worked. With all the cameras I planted I was able to find the perfect time to get you here…"

Cameras?

Boss stood up and walked towards the window.

"I used your card and bought the plan ticket hoping you would take the trip. I feared you wouldn't, but it was risk I was willing to take. Let me say I heard you talking yourself out of it a few times, but finally you gave in and came right to me. I had to be discreet Blair; you aren't like the others. They were thrown out on the street or were washed up nobodies. They were easy to take without leaving a trail where people would miss them. You had made a name for yourself, so it made things a challenge. Not only that but don't you see the irony in it all. You went from saving animals to being the animal that needs to be saved. I must say I never thought you would live this long here but you have proven me wrong…"

Turning away from the window he faced me.

"You are special. I have just one more gift for you."

Slowly he turned and walked to the door. In a swift motion he tapped on the door three times. The door opened, and my heart picked up speed. It was nerve-racking to wait and see what or who came through the door. I wanted to run from fear. Trust was a strong word and there was no way I trusted him even a little bit. Footsteps came from outside the door and a figure finally appeared in the door way. "Impossible…"

That was the only word I could mutter at that time.

CHAPTER TEN

With my mouth covered, tears started to flow down my cheeks. I couldn't force my feet to move even an inch. My body trembled, I was dizzy and lightheaded, and my stomach started to hurt. My eyes became blurry as I wondered if I was imagining things. There in the doorway was my mother; the woman who had been missing for four long years. So many questions ran through my mind all at once but none of them made their way out. *How? When? Why?*

Forcing my feet to move I made my way to my mother. She stood still with tears running down her face. Something was different with her and I instantly worried for her safety. She looked at Boss, who stood nearby, as if asking for permission. A quick nod from him sent my mother's feet moving in my direction. It only took seconds for her to hug me tight. Sobbing was an understatement because at that moment I was losing it in my mother's arms. She pushed me arm's length away and held my face in her hands.

"It's you Blair, my god it's really you."

I looked into her eyes and nodded. So much pain showed in my mother's face and it hurt my heart.

"Why are you here Mama? Are you okay? Have they done anything to hurt you?"

My mother shook her head and looked back at Boss as I gave him a go to hell look.

"Can I please sit with her and explain things?"

With a stern look on his face, he nodded his head and started for the door.

"Mia, you have ten minutes and then you have to get back to your duties. The hunters will be hungry soon so make it fast."

The door shut behind him and my mother sat down on the bed. She patted the bed in a soft gesture and I sat down by her.

"Baby girl I don't have much time so let me hurry. I was taken one night when I got into a fight with your father. I went to the store and someone grabbed me from behind. The next thing I remember was waking up in a car blindfolded. I was brought to this house and given rules of what to do. I was to be a nurse to those who needed it and a maid for the hunters. I was to take care of anyone who won the three-day prize and make sure the house was looked after for Boss. I kept a hidden diary under my pillow and one night he found it. He used it against me and swore he would find you. I guess you could say it is my fault you were chosen. I wrote about how active and how head strong you are. Before I knew it, you were here in this bed. I never knew you were here until I was told someone won the prize. I came in expecting someone else and was given you instead. After I cleaned you up and took care of all the wounds Boss rushed me out as if he wouldn't let me see you again."

My mother ran her hand across my face to where some of the bandages were.

"My God Blair, what did they do to you?"

With my heart aching I looked away in embarrassment. It hurt to have my mother see me like that.

"I am fine Mama. Right now, I need you to tell me all you can about how they run the lands okay?"

We sat and talked, and I gathered all the information I could from my mother. With a plan slowly developing in my mind I enjoyed my stay inside. Food was brought to me three times that day. Each time my mother brought me food she and I were given ten minutes. For that I was thankful. Many years had passed, but I never gave up hope that she was alive.

New bandages were applied that night. Though I was in a comfortable bed, sleep didn't come to me much. My mind was so focused on my mother being alive and forming an escape plan that I couldn't turn off my thoughts. Boss never visited me again that day, but I knew he would be back the next day. My gut also told me that I wouldn't be able to get the prize again. Though it was true that Boss hadn't lied to me, I still didn't trust him. Deep down I knew he was a sick man trying to earn my trust, so he could kill me once I let my guard down. I was determined to not let that happen.

****

I was awaken by the sun slightly shinning in the window again. A knock on the door followed shortly. I jumped up with excitement looking forward to seeing my mother. She was the only thing that kept me going and seeing her face gave me hope. Opening the door, I instantly regretted my excitement. There Boss stood in the doorway. He was dressed to impress in a grey suit and a black tie, his hair was cut short, and his blue eyes shined as he strolled in with a black duffle bag in his hand. Leaving the door opened I walked back to the bed and sat down. I kept my eyes on him as he walked to the bed. He sat the bag down and then walked to the corner of the room and sat in the chair.

"Open the bag and choose which item you would like as your prize."

With shaky hands I reached in the bag and pulled out the four items. I laid them each on the bed and carefully thought about each one. The first item was a flashlight. I instantly checked it off the list, because it would only attract the hunters to where I was if the hunt went longer than daylight. The second item was a water bottle with water inside it. It was questionable at that point because I could always use water. The question was how loud it would be in the woods. I knew it would give my location away with just one plastic pop. The next item was shoes. It was also questionable because of the tracks it would leave. The last item was a protein bar. If I chose it then I could eat it in my cage before the hunt but then again, I didn't know when I was given the items.

"When do I get these items? Do I get them the instant I leave here and am placed back inside my cage?"

Boss folded his hands over each other and said, "No, you don't leave here with them and go to your cage. You are given them before you start your hunt, in front of the hunters."

If that's the case, the protein bar would be too loud and draw attention to me.

The more I thought about the items the more I realized they were for the hunter's advantage and not mine. Either way I had to choose something or else he would catch on to me and my thoughts. The most logical thought was to go with the flashlight. If I had to I could hit someone with it. With his eyes watching my every move I picked up the flashlight.

I looked him directly in his eyes and said, "I choose the flashlight as my prize."

With a smirk on his face he walked over to me and placed all the items back in the bag.

"Mia will be in soon to feed you. You will sleep here tonight and be taken back to your cage in the morning."

With that he walked out of the room and closed the door behind him. Many thoughts ran through my mind and I wondered if I made the right choice. It didn't matter because my choice was made, and I would have to live with it.

The rest of the day was nice, because I got to see my mother. However, that night I didn't sleep and remained in my bed thinking. I would go back to the cage the following morning and my battle would start all over.

CHAPTER ELEVEN

The next morning, I watched the sun come up. That not only meant I would be sent back to my cage, but that I would have to say my final goodbye to my mother. A knock on the door came and my mother walked in. A tear ran down my cheek as I watched her walk towards me. Knowing that I could die or get her killed by trying to escape put a heavy strain on my heart. However, if I didn't try I would die anyway and eventually my mother would die as well.

"Blair don't cry or you're going to make me cry. It is going to be okay baby girl."

She was always the positive one of the family and made sure in the worst times to be the light for everyone. It amazed me that my mother could be so hopeful in such a shit hole of a place.

"Mama, I just want you to know I love you so much. I am not going out without a fight and I will do my best for you."

"Blair, all I've ever known was you to doing your best at everything you do. You have done that and so much more. I love you sweet girl and I am so proud of everything you have ever done with your life. Please know how much I love you."

A tear ran down my mother's cheek and I wiped it away. Embracing her in a hug, no other words were spoken. A knock on the door caused me to jump. In walked Boss with a taller guy behind him. It was time for her to leave and for me to go back to my cage.

"It's time to go 2-9-6-5. Take your robe off and come with us," Boss said.

Hugging my mother one last time I watched her walk out of the room. Slowly I dropped my robe and walked to the door already putting my mind in fight mode.

"If you can walk to the cage without fighting, Jeff won't drag you by your hair. Do you think you can do that?"

With a head nod I followed Jeff out of the room and down some stairs. When I was brought into the house I was passed out, so that was the first time I was seeing the house. It smelled like herbs and food, and was warm with a cool breeze flowing through it. At the bottom of the stairs it was all open. The ceilings were taller than I would have imagined and windows stretched from bottom to top. Everything else was white including the furniture and carpet. Couches were set in the middle of the room in a square shape with a square coffee table in the middle. Hunters sat around the table on the couches with their eyes glued on me.

Locking eyes with as many as I could, I gave them a devil's stare. Plans of my escape ran through my mind looking at them. They must have seen the anger in me because they looked down at the floor. Jeff nudged my shoulder and I started to follow him again. After reaching the door I could see the sun in the distance slowly coming up. Stopping outside of the door, Jeff looked at me.

"Take off all the bandages and hand them to me."

Rolling my eyes, I slowly took off all my bandages and passed them over to him. It took a while because I was covered from head to toe with them. When I was fully naked, Jeff walked away, and I followed behind him. Once at my cage I crawled inside and sat down.

A little while later an alarm caused me to jump and instantly my heart started to beat. The sun was fully up and it was starting to get hot. It was happening all over again and this time the ending would be different. I only hoped I would be picked for the hunt. Boss' annoying voice came over the speaker and I couldn't help but roll my eyes. Reluctantly I listened to his annoying announcements.

Pain and anger was building inside me as I gained so many reasons to want him dead; the racist comments, having people hunt me like an animal, having me beaten almost to death, kidnapping me, and finally, holding my mother as a prisoner for four years. Death would come to him and I would see to it that it happened.

Shaking the morbid thoughts of me killing Boss slowly from my mind, I sat still and focused on the numbers being called. Rocking back and forth I hoped my number would be called. Sure enough the last number on the list to be called was mine. It was a number I came to hate, but that would always be a part of me because of the branding on my leg. Pushing my hand through the bars I waited to be jerked out of the cage. It shocked me when the door opened and no one reached in to drag me out by my hair. Quickly I crawled out of the cage and followed the man to the line. The others were pulled by their hair and thrown in line. A light went off in my mind and I knew what they were doing. I was a prize. Boss wanted the hunters to know it as well as the others being hunted. Boss was isolating me, so the others would hate me and also want me dead. With special treatment under my belt it put two sets of targets on my head. It wasn't a good feeling, but I would deal with it the best I could. Hunters watched me like a hawk and the others gave me a look of disgust. A deep arrogant laugh came from Boss.

It was go time and I had a mission to do. Stretching my legs out I kept my eyes down on the ground as Boss walked over to me. I stood up to face him. Without saying a word, he handed me the flashlight I had chosen the day before. With steady hands I took it from him and went back to stretching. Listening to his every word I waited for the right time to stop stretching.

Boss explained the rules to the others and the new batch of hunters. Though they were old news to me, I still listened. Once the rules were read off I stood up straight and got ready to run. With my heart beating fast I took off the instant he yelled run. It was time to show everyone who the real boss was and get the hell out of his place.

Like a fire had been lit under me I took off into the woods and traveled the same way I had the first day. The field was my goal and I had twenty minutes to get into position. With most of my wounds healing I was feeling almost brand new. It was crazy how my feet seemed to be used to the rough ground under them and my body didn't take notice to any branches swinging out hitting me. A burning grew inside me like never before and I felt a positive energy surging over my body. The only word I could find to explain it was determination.

Jumping over roots and splashing through puddles I ran harder than I had before. Ten minutes had passed, and I had already reached the field. With time on my side I started to cover myself in mud and grass. The sun was blocked by clouds and it looked like rain would come soon. It was bad weather to most people but perfect for me. A running noise startled me. Knowing it was too fast to be a hunter, I looked for one of the others. Soon my eyes found him, and it was the man who had talked to me from the cage near mine. Stopping in his tracks he ran towards me. It was my only chance to get someone else on my side and I hoped he didn't hate me as much as the others seemed to. In a low whisper he finally spoke.

"What are you doing?"

With a smiled I looked at him.

"Getting in position to kill all these bastards and get everyone out of here. You can help me by getting some others to ban together with us. We can overpower them and get off this god forsaken land."

His eyes gave his emotions away. I knew he was hesitant about my plan, but a small spark in him gave me some hope.

"What makes you so sure that we can even pull it off? They have us like rats in a cage."

He was right, but I had to try to explain it to him.

"Look I know what you are saying is right, but

let's be honest. How long can you keep doing this before you break? Once you break you will either give up or get stupid and die. It's now or never. Trust me. No matter what we do we will die if we don't try."

Deep brown eyes stared back at me and I had no clue which way he would go. With me holding my breath he finally spoke.

"Okay, but we don't have much time before they come for us. Tell me what to do."

With all the plans laid out the man shot off into the thick tress. It was my turn to do my part. Gritting my teeth, I laid on my stomach and army crawled through the field positioning myself to where I could see anything coming from the tree line. The mud soaked into my healing cuts on my front side and burned a little. Scabs were being pulled off my body as I slid across the ground, but it was game time and I was ready.

CHAPTER TWELVE

A good while and a few hundred bug bites later, I finally heard soft footsteps. With my heart beating in my brain I tried to calm my body. It wasn't as easy as it had been prior because I was going to be risking my life like never before. It was a good thing my father taught me how to whistle because I was going to need that skill. In as normal of a tone as I could muster up I whistled. The footsteps immediately stopped. After a few seconds the steps picked back up and were moving slowly toward me. Leaves crunched and a small sniffle let me know he wasn't far away from me at all. If my heart could jump out of my chest it would have in that moment. Taking someone's life was never on my list of ''to dos,'' but it was them or me. None of the skills I had learned prepared me for that moment. With all the rescued animals I saved I was able to run from a hunter. Being tough gave me the strength to take all the wounds I had endured but nothing could prepare me to kill another human being.

Pushing my wild thoughts aside I focused on the sound of the footsteps. Suddenly a glimpse of a boot came into my view through the tall thick moving grass. I hoped he would turn his back to me, so I could make my move. My nerves were getting to me and by then I was sweating. Pacing my breathing I waited for the right time to strike. When he eventually walked past me, I knew I wouldn't have another chance. Quietly I got up, so he wouldn't hear me coming. With the flashlight in my right hand and my left hand balled up in a fist I pulled my right hand back and swung as hard as I could. The flashlight hit him against the side of his head and his body went limp falling to the ground. Grabbing the gun from the ground, quickly I aimed it at his body. I knew I had to hurry because I was in an open field and wouldn't have long before someone could spot me. The fear inside me turned to anger knowing that he was going to kill me just minutes before. Taking the safety off of the gun, I pointed it at his heart and pulled the trigger. A shot rang out and an abnormal feeling washed over me.

There was no turning back and I had six more men to go through before the hard part really began.

Doing my best with my wounded body I pulled him back into the woods. A sudden thought hit my mind and I raced back out into the field to grab my flashlight. With an evil smile I stripped the hunter of his clothes and put them all on. They were baggy on me, but they would work for the time being. Doing my best, I covered the man with mud from head to toe. I rolled him over face down on the ground to make him look like one of the people being hunted.

The tables had turned, and I had become the hunter. With hunting clothes on and the hood pulled up over my head, I went on the search for more hunters. On my arm was a blue ribbon and I figured it was how they color coated each other to know who was who. Playing the part, I kept the gun out and pointed all around as if hunting. My next problem was each hunter was only given one bullet. I already used his bullet and had to figure out how to kill the next hunter. Looking down at the oversized shoes on my feet, I tried to figure out a new plan.

Suddenly a branch broke nearby. I looked in

the direction of the noise. Crouching next to a tree was one of the others. Laying my gun down I looked around to make sure no one else was around. Once I knew it was safe I pushed my hood back to show my face. The man's eyes changed from fear to shock. In a crab walking motion, he hobbled over to me. I kneeled down to his level and he grabbed my face smiling. I could tell he couldn't speak English, but words were not needed for us to speak. He knew my plan just from looking at me and laid down flat on the ground as if he was dead. Looking up at me he smiled and gave me a thumbs up. A new plan was in motion and this time I had help.

Just as I grabbed my gun, stood back up, and put my hood back on, I heard footsteps come from behind me. It had to be another hunter because they were slow and swift. Looking down in the man's eyes below me I held my finger to my lips to tell him to remain quiet. Keeping my back to the noise was the hardest part, but I couldn't give my face away. I had to be patient and wait for him to come to me as I aimed the gun down as if I had just shot the man on the ground.

My blood was pumping, and my mind was racing through all the things that could possibly go wrong. I waited for my next move. Letting my mind quiet down I focused on the steps that were even closer to me. The man below me stayed still if he was dead. Visions of my mother flashed in my mind and I knew she was one of the many reasons I was killing these people. Someone had to die, and it wouldn't be me or her. The sick bastards wanted to play a sick game of cat and mouse and I was going to give it to them, just not the way they intended it to be played.

"Robert, did you get that girl or was it one of the others?"

The man's voice was a whisper, so I knew he was close. His breathing was loud, and I could tell he was out of breath.

"Robert, you can't shoot anyone else but the girl! Rich will be pissed if we shoot any of the others before she is shot, you should know this."

Just as I felt him grab my shoulder I turned to face the monster. With wide eyes he pulled a shaky hand away from me and reached for his gun. Anger rushed through me, and I took the gun in my hand and swung it around as fast as I could hitting him in the head with the barrel. He fell to the ground and blood oozed out of his head. The guy that was once lying on the ground jumped up next to me and reached for the hunter's gun.

Instantly I pushed him back and tried to communicate with him the best I could.

Speaking slowly I said, "He is already dead. Don't waste the bullet. Dead. He is dead."

I tried to use my hands to point and show him what I meant. Bending over I put two fingers on the hunter's neck, but no pulse was there. Shaking my head I hoped he understood me. The man nodded his head and stood up to keep watch. As quickly as I could I stripped the hunter of his clothes and handed them to the man. While he was getting dressed I turned the hunter over and covered him with mud and leaves. Then I took the gun with the bullet and handed the man the gun that was empty.

I took a second to think. The hunter said something of importance. They weren't supposed to shoot anyone until I was dead. That meant my shot triggered the hunters to really begin hunting. That wasn't my only thought though. We were all equipped with GPS devices in our arms and that meant we couldn't travel together. They would begin to notice it once we travelled in groups.

Staying low key meant the world to my plan. Trying my best I used my hands again to try to explain to the man that we should split up. Even saying it out loud in case he could understand me.

"We have to separate. They are tracking us. Find and kill as many as you can."

He nodded his head as if he understood and then took off walking slowly in the opposite direction. If we could get others to join in, then it would make my plan easier on me. Shifting my weight to my less injured side I began to walk on. The once healed wounds on my body were starting to hurt again and I wasn't sure how bad the pain would become. Deciding to take things slow was my best option in the long run. Plus, hunters didn't move fast, and they would know something was off if I was running around.

The sun was high in the sky and two hunters were down leaving only five left. That was if the other guy hadn't killed anyone else. Just as the thought crossed my mind a shot rang out and nervousness reached my stomach. It put a lot of fear inside me because if the guy got caught then my whole plan could be blown.

I made my way to the water. I leaned down, so I could get a drink before pressing forward on my hunt. I noticed a little boy hiding inside a bush. He couldn't have been more than fourteen or so and I knew he was scared. I stopped and decided to let him know what I was doing. It was the least I could do to tell him to lay low and be safe. Signing to him to be quiet, I moved in his direction.

When I got over to him I crouched down to where I could see his face. There was no way I would involve a teenager into my whirlwind plan. I would never be able to live with myself if a kid got hurt because of my crazy ass mind.

As quiet as I could I whispered to him, "Can you speak English?"

He was shaking and a tear ran down his face. It took everything in me not to get closer and embrace him in a hug. Eventually he shook out a nod.

"Okay good. You don't have to talk but listen to me okay?"

Another shaky nod followed.

"I am going to get us all out of here safe or at least I'm going to die trying. You need to lay low and hide as good as you can okay? There is another man helping me, but I don't want you to get hurt so just stay quiet and hide."

All the boy did was nod his head and look at me with sad eyes. Something stuck me in the back and caused me to understand just why he was shaking. It wasn't because he was afraid of me, it was because another hunter was behind me. My time was up and everything I worked for was coming to an end.

CHAPTER THIRTEEN

"Get up. Now!"

His voice was deep, but I could hear uneasiness in his tone. It was just the edge I needed to put my mind into motion. Slowly I stood up with the gun in my left hand and my right hand in a tight fist. A bead of sweat ran down my spine into my wounds and burned. It only reminded me why I was fighting so hard to live. Looking the boy in the eyes I saw all the fears he had.

"Turn around slowly and then put the gun on the ground," the man said in a steadier voice.

I turned my body and bent over to lay the gun down. As the barrel of his gun followed me to the ground, I knew I had to do something quick. I jumped up and aimed my gun at him. I knew there was a fifty-fifty chance that he would shoot me when I moved so fast, but it was a chance I was willing to take. Luck was on my side because he didn't shoot and just stood there with big eyes staring at me.

"Each of our guns are only given one bullet woman and I'm pretty sure you used yours. So, if you are smart you would do what I say."

It shocked me how fearless I was in that moment. That could have been the moment I died, but fear was nowhere to be found. A smirk ran across my face.

"Let me show you how smart I am," I said as I pulled the trigger.

The shot rang out and the man fell backwards. I dropped the gun, and turned to the boy who was crying and rocking back and forth.

"It's okay. I am okay and so are you. Now help me so we can get you dressed. We have to hurry."

Leaning over to the man I shot, I started to undress him. Undoing the buttons on his jacket I felt something grab my arm.

"He will kill you. You won't escape this place.

We didn't have a choice either. It was you or us."

I pushed his hand off of me and asked, "What do you mean, you didn't have a choice either?"

"It was our decision to come here and hunt, but we had no idea what we were hunting…We…We paid for the trip and all the things they provided but…When we found out we were hunting people…They told us we either did it or died."

Shock rocked my mind as I waited for him to talk. He was struggling to get words out.

"My guess…is they would force us to hunt you and if we told anyone…we would be charged with the crime and not them…Either way you won't leave the land…They will kill you."

Looking him in the face I made sure he could see just how determined I was.

"I WILL get off this land and I WILL do it alive. Too bad you won't be alive to see it."

A loud gargle came out and he took his last breath. As I took his clothes off many thoughts crossed my mind. *They were forced to hunt us and we were forced to be hunted. They were hunting for their lives and we were running for ours.* It was a sick twisted game, but it only made the do or die situation worse.

I handed the boy the clothes and watched him put them on. They didn't fit but he didn't seem to mind.

"Okay I am going to give you the empty gun and I will take the loaded one. All you have to do is walk around and look like one of the hunters."

With a nod he leaned down and tied up the shoes. Once he stood up he looked in my eyes.

"What do I do now? How would I know when I'm safe?"

"Do you know where the field is that meets the big hill?"

He gave me another head nod.

"Go there and stay close to that area. Once I am done I will meet you there and help you get the GPS out of your arm. Try to stay quiet and not let any of the other hunters get too close to you. If they do get close to you, then you fight for your life. Just remember they have a loaded gun. Don't be a hero, but don't let them kill you. There are others like us who are dressed in hunting clothes too. Be careful because they won't know you are one of us. Just stay quiet and keep low."

He nodded his head again and I was off.

I made my way through the woods. My next stop was the bushes because it was one of the places hunters hated to visit but didn't have any other choice to. It gave the others perfect coverage from the hunters and if I were a hunter that's where I would look. The plan was in motion and, three others were on board with the plan. I could only hope it was going good for them as well.

Crossing the shallow creek, I stopped dead in my tracks because I thought I heard someone. I had only killed three hunters and if I kept going that meant I had four more to go. My mind was playing tricks on me, because no one was there. My body started to scream at me and I knew I would have to slow down even if just for a little bit. Though my wounds were healing, I wasn't anywhere near the best of health. Sweat was getting in the open cuts and they were burning, and my ankle was starting to swell. The clothes on my body were rubbing against the open wounds from the thorns. Even without the thorns in my body it still hurt to have anything touch the holes where they once were.

The sun was gone, and clouds completely covered the sky. Rain started to fall, and the air was humid. The smell of wet leaves and mud hit my nose. It was a smell that I loved as a child, but it was becoming a smell I hated. Sweat mixed with dirt and mud ran down my face into my eyes. Rubbing my eyes only made it worse because my hands were dirty as well.

Finally, I reached the edge of the bushes. Before I entered I waited to see if I could hear anyone else. Someone coughed and got my attention behind me. I hoped it wasn't another hunter. When I turned around I saw it was the guy from the cage next to mine. I was glad he hadn't tried to kill me and noticed it was me and not another hunter. Slowly I walked over to him.

I crouched down to his level and he whispered, "How many have you killed?"

I kept my voice in a whisper along with his and I spoke softly, "So far three and I have two others in hunting uniforms. What about you? I shot twice, but heard another shot. Was that you?"

"I only killed one and that was with my hands. He shot at me but missed so I guess that's the shot you heard. I can't believe you heard it because we were on the other side of the lands. That leaves us with only three more to go, unless the others have killed some."

Shaking my head, I looked at my feet.

"I don't think they will kill any of the hunters, but I could be wrong. I told them to lay low and play the part."

The man looked down at the gun in my hand.

"Does that have a bullet in it or did you use it?"

"I didn't use this one, so I have one left. We are close to ending this and we can't stop now. Did you find the others and let them know what to do?"

He nodded his head.

"We have to split up. The GPS will pick us up here together and we can't let that happen for too long."

"Okay. Which way are you going?"

I pointed to the thick bushes.

"Be careful. I saw two hunters go in together not long ago and without a bullet I wasn't about to try to take them both. Can you handle them while I try to find the last one?"

With a firm nod I stood up and walked to the bush line. Taking a deep breath, I entered the thick bushes and made my way forward. With every step I took I paused before taking another one. With my thoughts clear I listened for any and everything. It was two against one and I had to be in the right state of mind. It was a state of mind no one ever wanted to experience because it was do or die. With your life on the line you do what you can to not die.

CHAPTER FOURTEEN

Mistakes weren't on my list of things to do and I had to make sure the only people making mistakes were the hunters. It began to drizzle and the rain made it hard to hear anything around me. It made me have to focus more. With the sun gone, there was no way to tell what time it was. I could only hope it wasn't close to the twelve hours. Twelve hours ended the hunt and would ruin my whole efforts up until that point.

A bush moved off in the distance to my right and caught my attention. A purple band shined, from the arm of a hunter. Another colored banned flashed and I knew both of them were in one spot. They were hunting together, which made killing them hard. I had to make a bold move. Pulling the gun up I aimed in the direction of the hunters and waited for one of them to step out enough to get a shot off. Slowing my breathing and trying to calm my adrenaline, I waited patiently. The purple armed man stepped out just enough for a good shot. Letting my deep breath out I pulled the trigger. Not even checking to see if it made its mark I crouched down and moved away. I feared they would figure out the direction of the shot, so I had to move. The bushes were familiar to me, so I had a little edge on the other hunter.

"Fuck! James! No!"

The hunter's voice let me know I had hit my target. Reaching down I took my shoes off and laid them under a bush. Being quiet and fast was important, and I couldn't do that with oversized shoes on. As fast and quiet as I could I circled them and made it to their backside. The other hunter was crouched down at the dead or dying hunter's side. With the gun in my hand, I made my move. I was out of bullets, but I still had the gun to make use of.

With only less than ten feet between us I jumped up and ran for it. Holding the gun over my head I swung it down on his face, like a baseball bat hitting a baseball. A loud crack came from his neck letting me know I broke it. The connection was made with so much force that I cracked the butt of the gun and jammed my wrist. It hurt like hell, but two hunters were dead and there was only one left. Reaching down with my good hand I picked up both of the guns. I was happy to see that they each had a bullet in them.

Striping the hunters down, I hid their clothes under the bushes and took the smaller man's shoes. After I rubbed mud on them and rolled them over face down I set off to get out of the bushes. When I reached the lining of the bushes I met the man again. He was out of breath and looked scared.

"Are you okay?"

He nodded his head and then walked over to me gripping a gun tight.

"The other hunter is dead. Did you kill the other two? I only heard one shot and came as fast as I could."

"They are both dead and I covered them up to look like one of us. Here, take this gun. We can give another prisoner one."

Catching his breath, he sat down on the ground.

"Now, we have to get the GPSs out of our

arms. Then head up to the main land."

The man's eyes got big and he started to shake his head.

"No. We have the advantage and we should run for help. We could get enough of a lead on them before they know what's going on and get someone to help us."

Though I didn't want to admit it, I knew he was right.

"Okay, let's get this out of our arms and meet up with the others."

We worked on each other with sharp sticks. Eventually we got them out of our arms and headed for the field. Two men in camouflaged sweat shirts stood at the edge of the field. We walked over to them and helped them get the devices out of their arms. The man handed one of them a loaded gun. Instantly they started to run, but my feet refused to move.

"What are you doing? We have to go now," the man yelled back at me.

"Look, my mother is back in that shit hole and I can't leave her. You three run off and get help but I have to go back for her. When they find out what we did they will kill her, I just know it."

Looking down at the ground I waited for him to speak.

"I understand. Here take this bullet out of the gun and keep it with you. It might come in handy. Stay strong and do what you have to. We will be back with help. I promise."

A feeling of relief came over me and I reached up and hugged the man. Before I could blink he was running away in the distance with the others and I was running back to the hell hole. With the advantage of them not knowing I was coming I hoped I could get my mother out safely.

Once the tree line was in my sight I slowed down to catch my breath and formulate my plan. I knew from the information I got from my mother that there were at least two guards at the cages, three men rode out on the four-wheelers to collect the bodies, and two guards at the house. The rain was pouring down by then, and it made it hard to see or hear anything. I had a plan in mind, but the hardest part of the plan was waiting. There was no way of knowing what time it was, so I had no clue how long I would be waiting. The three men would eventually come out on the four-wheeler and that's when I would make my move. It was the only option I had to go with that would keep the numbers down. While the three men were out collecting bodies, I planned on sneaking up to the cages and killing the two guards. I would have to use my hands because the gun would alarm the other guards at the house. The only worry I had was if they would know something was wrong because seven shots never rang out. They would have to go get them because the twelve-hour limit was up. I was only there a few days, so I didn't know if that ever happened before. It wouldn't take long for the people on the four-wheelers to figure out what was going on and come back to report it. Again, time wasn't on my side, so I had to move fast.

I sat against a tree and waited for the sound of the four-wheelers. The rain didn't show any signs of letting up. However, I was thankful for it. It would give me coverage when I moved and also hide any noise I made. As I leaned on the tree, the rain started to get harder and made seeing almost impossible. Not only was seeing difficult, but I wasn't able to hear either. Closing my eyes, I focused on my ears as much as I could. It felt good to close my eyes because I was so tired, but sleep wasn't an option. Sitting still made my adrenaline high start to fade. I knew that if I didn't move I would crash. My body had been running constantly and I wasn't sure how long it would last. I almost gave up on waiting and jumped the gun to get things started, but a soft rumble in the distance stopped me. Sitting up I opened my eyes and focused on what I was hearing; hoping it wasn't thunder that I heard. Another rumble started up and I knew they were coming. A bolt of adrenaline shot through me. Lights shined just above me over the hill where the cages were. Sliding down I laid flat on the ground and hoped they didn't see me or worst, run me over. The noise of the four-wheelers grew along with the rain. They were close, and I could feel myself holding my breath. All my efforts up until that point were weighing on them passing me by.

Suddenly dirt flew, and lights came my way. The engine of the four-wheeler flew over me as they jumped the hill and passed by me. The last one almost landed on top of me; needless to say I almost shit bricks. Letting out a breath I waited until I couldn't see their lights anymore. If I couldn't see them then I knew they couldn't see me. I jumped up and made my way out of the tree line. Darting across the opening I made my way to the side of the building that held the cages.

I crouched down and started to take my clothes off. I couldn't move like I wanted to in the clothes and I also needed to blend in with the others that were in the cages. With the gun still in my hand I decided to lay it down and cover it with the clothes. Eventually I would need it, but not at that moment. In a slow motion I looked around the corner to see where the guards were standing. They were both at the far end under the roof where the cages sat. They were talking; giving me the advantage I needed. After I got in the building without being seen, I had to split them up somehow. An idea came to mind and a new form of hope ran through me. Pulling my head back I leaned against the building.

"You can do this Blair. We are almost through this," I said to myself.

Speaking to myself out loud wasn't uncommon. I needed a pick me up and no one else was around to give me one. Closing my eyes, I took a deep breath in and let it out. A vision of my mother flashed in my mind and made me smile.

"We will get through this. Tell me what to do."

My heart skipped a beat and my eyes flew open. There in front of me was the guy from the cage near mine.

"You were supposed to go for help with the others. You shouldn't be here. You were free why the hell would you come back?"

A smile crossed his face.

"I couldn't let you do this alone. I turned back not long after I caught up to the other guys. I told them to go get help and come back for us. After the rain started up I used it as coverage and hunkered down near the cages. I saw you run across the field and came to meet you here. So, what's the plan Blair?"

Shock ran through my mind, but I was grateful for his help.

"There are two guards out here and two at the house; one inside the house and one outside. Then there is Boss and my mother inside. We also have the three men on four-wheelers to worry about when they come back."

A sly grin crossed his face and I couldn't help but feel confused.

"I don't think we will have to worry about the men on the four wheelers. The others are helping take care of them. Have you seen where these two guards are at?"

"They are huddled inside from the rain talking to each other on the far end. First, we will have to separate them. We should move while it's raining hard to help mask our sounds."

"I have an idea," the man said.

"Okay cool," I said before the man quietly shared his idea with me.

We quickly made our way inside the building towards the back where the wall was. We had to stay out of sight and creep up behind them. Staying low I watched as he made his way to the far end. Eyes followed us from all the nearby cages. Curious dirty faces stared at me as I waited for him to take his spot. A girl around my age was in the cage closest to me. Fear was in her eyes and sadness on her face. In a soft whisper I spoke to her hoping she could understand me.

"Do you speak English?"

A nod followed my question.

"I need your help to get the guard's attention. Do you think you could do that for me?"

It took a minute, but another nod came.

"When I moved down three cages I need you to make some noise. Start talking and get one of them to come to the cage. I know that they hurt people who speak while in the cages, but don't worry I promise they won't hurt you. I plan to get us all out of here okay?"

The girl didn't nod, and I worried I would have to find another person to do the deed. Something changed in her eyes as I started to move away. Through the bars the girl grabbed my arm to prevent me from moving. She slowly nodded her head and looked down at the other cages. I made my move and waited for her to set off the alarm for one of the guards to make his way down to her. With my heart racing I knew I had to keep my promise and not let her get hurt no matter what.

CHAPTER FIFTEEN

The girl started talking to the person in the cage next to her. I couldn't make out her words, but it was clear she was talking. One of the guards mumbled and started walking towards the cage. It was show time. I gave one last look to the end of the cages at the man. He was crouched down looking at me and waiting for the right timing. The guard came into view and I waited for him to get a little closer to the girl's cage. Once I saw him pull out a cattle prod I stood up and made my move. Running, I threw my naked body at him, forcing him to the floor. It was one wrestling match I had to win. With a ton of force, he punched me in the stomach and I felt my air leave my body. Instantly I fired back and punched him in the temple. My weak punch didn't do enough damage and I could see the anger in his eyes. It was time for me to unleash holy hell on him. Drawing back, I used both hands and scratched his face and neck.

Suddenly I felt his hands around my neck squeezing. His grip got tighter, and I had to think fast. The only advantage I had on him was being on top of him. Pulling my knee up, I pushed it as hard as I could down on his crotch. An awful sound came out of his mouth and I knew it was working. Using all my body weight I picked up my knee and slammed it back down on his package. It was just enough for him to let one hand off my neck. Quickly I pulled his other hand off my neck and bit his arm. I used enough force to draw blood. In a swift motion I rolled off of him and grabbed the cattle prod he dropped. I pressed it to his neck and pushed the button. With that, I watched his eyes go from anger to pain with no remorse.

A glare from the flood light and a puddle showed me a rock the size of my fist on the ground. Reaching over him I grabbed it and began to slam it down on his head. I hit him over and over. I couldn't stop. Fear ran through me and I was scared he wouldn't be dead. *What if he's not dead and gets up to kill me?* It was me or him.

My name was called and I snapped out of my moment. My new found friend was standing there looking at me with sadness on his face. Dropping the rock, I rolled away from the bloody faced and apparently dead guard.

"Come on we have to keep going. Get the keys off his side and let's get some of these people out of here."

Snapping out of my shock, I grabbed the guard's keys and started unlocking cages. Once some of them were out I passed him the keys and turned my attention to the ones that were already out.

"I know most of you don't speak English. I need you to stay put until we kill the other two guards. Once we enter the house y'all can run away. Just don't go out of this building until we enter the house. Also stay quiet and out of sight. You need to keep in the mindset that you are still being hunted. We don't know what is waiting past the tree line. When you run make sure you find help."

Some of them nodded and others only smiled. It was a good feeling to know I had gotten them out of the cages and made it to that point of my plan.

Turning around, I looked the man in the eyes again.

"What is your name? You know my name from me talking to myself, but I don't know yours."

Shaking his head, I heard him chuckle under his breath a little.

"My name is Adam. I would have told you before, but it never seemed to be the right time."

I smiled and walked to the wall of the building that was closest to the house. There were only two guards and Boss standing in my way. The rain had started to let up, but not much. It was still good coverage for us so we needed to hurry before it stopped and made things harder for us. The guard was sitting under the awning near the front door to the house. There weren't any trees around the house to hide behind and the only coverage we had was rain and a bush planted right between the building and the house.

The guard didn't look to have a gun, so it was plus. We made our way to the bush. Adam patted my back and I let out a loud whistle. The guard shot up and looked around. With another pat to my back I did it again. Slowly the guard moved away from the door and walked towards the bush we were hiding behind. The only thing we didn't account for was a flashlight he turned on and shined our way. Holding our breath, we stayed as still as we could. With the guard only ten feet from the bush, Adam patted my back two more times. We jumped up and charged at the guard. Adam jumped on the guard's back and put him in a choke hold while I kicked the guy in his package. The guard fell to his knees and I picked up the flashlight he dropped. He started pulling at Adam's arms. I knew Adam couldn't hold on much longer because the guard was huge. I was thankful for Adam's help because I wouldn't have been able to take him alone. Pulling back the flashlight I swung it hard against the guard's face. One hit wasn't enough, so I kept going until his hands dropped from Adam's arms. Once he was knocked out, I helped Adam pull the guard's body back to the building and locked him in one of the cages. The guard would most likely die, but we didn't want to take a chance on him coming after us. Gathering my wits, I stood up next to Adam who was at the edge of the building looking at the house.

"What's wrong?"

Slowly, he turned and looked back me.

"Something just doesn't feel right about you

going inside. I can't put my finger on it. Shouldn't they have cameras or radios to talk back and forth? Could they really be that dumb to not have that technology?"

It was something I hadn't questioned myself and I couldn't help but feel Adam was right. It didn't matter either way because my focus was rescuing my mother.

"I don't know what's waiting behind that door, but I know I have to go in. You don't have to go with me Adam and I'm not going to ask you to. You have done more than I could have ever asked of anyone and for that I'm beyond grateful. I am going to go grab the gun I have and put the two bullets to use."

Quickly I walked away and went to grab my gun. All the others were out of the cages and standing against the wall waiting. As I walked past them they each touched my shoulder, patting it as if saying thank you. After grabbing my gun, I turned back to face all of them. No one spoke but they didn't have to. It was written on their faces that they thought I was going to die. Giving a small smile and a head nod I walked back to Adam.

"Okay Adam, stay with the others. Once I'm inside, get yourself and them to safety. Don't come back for me again Adam."

Without waiting for a response, I walked towards the house with my head held high. My heart was grateful to him and all he had done. As I moved forward towards the house, I couldn't help but feel as if I was walking to my death. If death was waiting for me on the other side of that door I would face it head on, proud of what I had accomplished. I took in a deep breath and let it out as I grabbed the door knob. With my gun in hand I opened the door ready to fight my final fight. However, what I found stopped me in my tracks.

CHAPTER SIXTEEN

Standing ten feet away from me was a guard with a gun pointed at me. As if that wasn't bad enough Boss was seated on the white couch smoking a cigar; with my mom on the floor between his legs. Her wrist was bond with rope and her mouth was duct taped. Adam was right; Boss was indeed waiting for me. It was hard to not let my emotions run rampant on me. Refusing to take my gun off the guard I kept my eyes wide and watched his every movement, while I also watched Boss out of the corner of my eye.

"Well hello Blair. How nice of you to stop in tonight."

The sound of his voice made me want to scream.

"Well you know…" I replied through clenched teeth.

Boss reached down beside my mother and grabbed a small glass from the table. After he took a sip of his drink, he let out a sigh and set the glass back down. My insides twitched when he leaned down and stroked my mother's face. I knew he was trying to make me angry and lose focus; something I knew I couldn't do if I wanted to survive. The guard inched my way. I kept my eyes on him only leaving little of my view to watch Boss.

"This woman you call mother is something else Blair," Boss said in his smug tone. "You see, you have no reason to be angry with me. It was your mother's fault that you ever came here to begin with," he added as he pulled her hair.

My mother let out a muffled scream. I didn't let his act shake me, because I knew he was hoping I'd move or flinch.

"This doesn't have to end this way. If you give me my mother, then I will walk away and never return."

A low evil chuckle that sent cold chills down my spine came out of his mouth. I knew he wouldn't go for it. My intent was to keep a conversation going so I could figure out my next move.

"You are a smart girl Blair. Playing dumb just isn't a good look for you. Allow me to explain a few things that might help clear things up for you, in case you care to know."

Good. Time was what I need. The others should have gotten help by now. Hopefully someone would come, I thought as he began talking.

"I started this land about twelve years ago. I will spare you too many detail because I know we don't have much time. When I started this land I wanted it to be for hunting rare animals. It wasn't until five years ago that I decided to use people instead of animals. At first hunters came willingly and were twisted enough to love the sport. They paid millions to be able to experience three days of killing people. As sick as you think it is, it was something they needed in order to live. They lived for killing people Blair..."

He took a drag of his cigar, before he continued talking.

"The bad thing about people who loved to kill

is they can't stop killing. They couldn't just kill people here; they wanted to kill people when they left the land. Eventually my regular customers started to get locked up for murder or killed themselves to prevent jail time. It got harder and harder to find people who enjoyed the idea of hunting humans. I could have gone back to rare animals, but what was the point? It had become something I loved just as much as the hunters who hunted the humans. I began to lie to them and make them sign a contract. They came thinking they were hunting animals and when they got here found out they were hunting humans."

He took another drag from the cigar and sat back against the couch.

"After a little while I noticed I needed someone to be a nurse, a maid, and my partner. I spent many months looking for the right person. Eventually a Google search led me to your lovely mother. She wasn't anything fancy, but was good at what she did. I couldn't risk getting someone famous or someone that would be missed too much. By a random draw your mother won this beautiful prize. It took a little while for Mia to act like she was supposed to, but we finally got on track. Her duties grew over the years, but she does them very well.

Anyway, life became normal, and I don't like normal. It was the same thing over and over every day. I needed a challenge and I was dying to find one. It was by chance that I found Mia's journal and once I read it I realized you were the challenge I needed."

Suddenly Boss stood up and walked to the kitchen.

"Would you like a drink Blair?"

The thought of something to drink sounded so good, but there was no way in hell I was taking anything from him.

"I'll take that as a no. Anyway, I gave it some thought and decided I had to have you here. There was a story behind you and your mother. You loved her so much and she loved you beyond words. Isn't that what you wrote Mia? Of course, I knew that you would be special but Blair... I had no idea you would be this special. In just a few days you managed to ruin everything I have worked for. You will be known as a hero for saving so many people. Something told me that when I brought you here it would be trouble, but I was ready for it. It wasn't easy to get you here away from everyone. I knew there was a chance you would try to get a refund for the plane ticket, but I took care of that too. Either way you fell for it and came right to me. Just like a fly to a spider's web."

After pouring himself a drink he walked back to the couch and sat down. Taking a sip of the drink, he set it down and put his cigar out in his old glass. It was my turn to speak and I was glad for him to shut up even if for a small amount of time.

"What do you want from us? It's over now, they are coming for you. Either they will kill you or take you to jail. So, what is the point of any of this?"

He stood up and walked towards me. I kept my eyes on the guard, refusing to look directly at Boss.

"Blair, you didn't let me finish. Now, as I was saying. Your mother has been such an immense help to me over the years. She even noticed when I became ill and has helped me in every way she could. Being an ill man, I honestly don't care how this ends. I am dying anyway so even if they come in and take me away I won't last much longer. My original hope was that you would shoot me and then the guard would kill you. However, I forgot how smart you were and you did not come in guns blazing."

Out of everything he'd said, the thing that stood out the most was the fact that he would die either way.

"Ahh you are wondering what's wrong with me, aren't you? Blair your mother diagnosed me with cancer a little over a year ago. Over time I have gotten worse and the last scan she did showed I don't have long to live. So, I could care less if I live or die. My life doesn't matter but I can see how much you and your mother's lives matter. You see, I'm not mad at what you have done Blair. Some of us may live and some may die. I'm just playing one last sick game with you."

He turned and walked over to the guard. Boss tapped him on the shoulder and the guard slowly handed Boss the gun. Boss moved back to the couch to sit down and the guard walked over to the kitchen.

"Now let's really get down to business, shall we? Jeff?"

"Yes Boss?" the guard responded.

"This is between Blair, Mia, and I so your assistance is no longer needed."

In a quick motion Boss held the gun up, aimed, and fired the gun at the guard. Shock once again rocked my body and adrenaline surged through my mind. When he shot the guard in the head my first thought was how good of an aim he had, and my second thought was me telling myself not to over think the first thought.

"Now Blair, I have a gun and you have a gun. I don't care if I live or die but you do. It's like an old western movie. Who will draw their gun first and who will fire the first shot?"

When he aimed the gun back at me, I felt like all my efforts were coming to an end.

"This is between you and me. Let my mother go and let's handle this like adults."

A smile came across his face that showed his white teeth and perfect smile.

"You're right. Mia, you may stand up and leave the room."

Not paying any attention to my mother I watched Boss' every move and twitch; searching for any indication that he would shoot my mother. Just as I let the thought cross my mind I seen him turn his head and squint his eyes in my mother's direction. In a split-second decision, I let out a breath and pulled the trigger. The shot ran out followed by another shot. As expected he shot his gun the instant I shot him. His gun flew out of his hands as his body fell to the ground. Keeping my gun aimed on him I walked to his side and kicked the gun away. With my hands shaking I held the gun with one hand and began to search my body with the other hand looking for bullet wounds.

When I didn't find any, I held the gun firmly in both hands and looked down at Boss. He was lying on the ground with a bullet wound in his chest looking up at me.

"I will die famous...I will forever be a part of your memory...My voice, name, and all the shit I put you through will haunt you forever...So even though I will die right here...You will never be able to get rid of me...Ever..."

Glad to have watched him take his last breath I turned to look for my mother. She was laid out on the ground. In that instant I realized he had shot her when I shot him. I dropped my gun and ran to her.

She had been shot in the arm. Obviously in shock, she laid there silently. I cradled her in my arms and checked her out. The bullet went right through her arm and thankfully it wasn't bleeding that bad. I heard sirens in the distance. I rocked her in my arms and waited for the police to come.

CHAPTER SEVENTEEN

One week later...

My mother and I were finally back at my house. Slowly we strolled to the front door, glad to finally be done with Angle Inlet. The FBI and local police wouldn't let us leave until we told them everything we knew. I couldn't give a lot information, but because my mother spent four long years on that land she knew more than anyone about the working of it.

We were questioned for seven long days before they allowed us to go home. However, while they drained all the information they could from us, I did the same to them. It turned out that Rich, "Boss," was forty-three years old and listed as a billionaire. That wasn't a shock to me because he'd said he made millions from all the hunters. Inside of a hidden room my mother told them about in the house, they found all his files. There were missing person reports from every person he brought to the land, as well as records and signed contracts from the hunters that had killed before. There wasn't a piece of paper that he didn't keep. Sadly, the paper work was all they had to go on because the bodies of all the people killed would never be found. It literally made me sick when I found out that the "dog food" they fed us was actually the remains of the other prisoners who were killed. The FBI found a burn pit on the land and plenty of ashes from bones.

They found records supporting the fact that the human hunts started five years prior. At the beginning they were only once a month, but increased every year until they were hunting almost every other day. It wasn't until I got on the land that they began hunting every day. Because of the detailed records, the FBI was able to start using the names from previous hunters and track them down. They promised they would charge each person they found with murder. They didn't seem to care that one of the hunters I had killed told me they were forced to kill them.

The first two days of being interrogated I was treated like a criminal. I understood because I did kill some of the hunters, guards, and Boss. Once my story aligned with the paperwork and my mother's information they began to understand why I did what I did. It was hard to relive everything over and over, but I had to tell them every small detail.

That day the others and I rescued sixty-three people from the cages. They were missing from all over the world and some had been there for months. The FBI said it would take a long time to talk to all the people who were kept as prisoners. The only question the FBI wouldn't answer for me was how many people were killed on the hunting land. I figured it was a number I probably didn't want to know anyway. Before we were sent back home they warned us about the media. We didn't want our names released, but they said eventually the media would catch up to us because people leaked information all the time. We agreed to not contact anyone until we got back home.

I unlocked my door and we walked inside; stopping in the living room. It felt foreign to be back home. Looking over at my mom I worried about her. Four years was a long time to be held prisoner. A knock came on the door. Out of habit my mother jumped up, placed her arms in a folded position behind her back, and walked to the door. It was part of her duties to always be on her toes when she was on the hunting land. With a tear running down her face she stopped in her tracks and looked back at me.

"I'm sorry Blair. I didn't mean to jump and try to get the door. I just...It is something I am used to."

"It's okay Mama."

My heart broke for my mother because I couldn't imagine the hell she went through over the years. I got up, I walked over to her, and hugged her tight.

"Mama go get something to drink and have a seat. You need to relax. The kitchen is right there."

With a nod my mother was off to the kitchen. I walked to the door and I looked out of the peep hole. Two officers stood at the door. After opening the door, I noticed they had duffle bags in their hands. My curiosity was peaked.

"Can I help you?"

"We are here to speak with Blair Saddler or

Mia Saddler."

Opening the door wider I folded my arms over my chest.

"I am Blair Saddler and my mother, Mia, is here as well."

I walked away from the door expecting they would follow me inside. Of course, they did.

"We are here to de-bug your home. The accused suspect left evidence that he bugged your home."

"Oh my god, yes!" I said as I brought my hands to my face. Deep flash backs came into my mind. "He told me that he hacked my laptop and placed cameras in my home. Please get them all before you leave."

Once back in the living room I found my mother on the couch sitting quietly.

"Mama these officers are here to de-bug the house. Let's leave so they can get the house cleared. We can go grab some food and get some fresh air."

She stood up and smiled at me, then followed me out of the house. We rode in silence most of the way to town. I couldn't help but think about how so many things were different with my mother. It was to be expected after being a prisoner and maid to someone else. There also wasn't any telling what else he made her do while she was there. It was something I planned to find out.

We pulled in at a local burger place and got out. The place was small, but they were known for their burgers and fries. Once we placed our order we sat at a booth far away from anyone else. I scanned the room. An older couple was seated near the entrance eating at a table for two. A mother and her red haired little girl were eating at the bar and I couldn't help but notice the girl pointing at the pie in the dish next to her. That made me smile. I looked over at my mother who was staring out the window into the traffic. I grabbed her hand and held it with mine.

"Mama talk to me. I went through a lot, but I know it doesn't compare to what you went through. I know it had to be bad. Please talk to me so I can help you."

She patted my hand with her free hand.

"Blair, that's the thing. It wasn't as awful as

you might think. I mean it was at first, but it got better with time."

She must have noticed my confused face because she sighed and looked back out the window. I knew she was about to pour here heart out to me and I was hoping I was ready to hear it.

"When they captured me, I was so scared. So many things ran through my mind; mainly the thought of the police blaming your father for me being missing. Possibly thinking your father hurt or even killed me seeing as we had such a huge fight just before. Then I worried about you and how you would live without me around.

At first, I thought they were going to kill me, but once I got to the land and they walked me past the cages into the house I knew something was different. They kept my hands bound behind my back but let me walk on my own. They never spoke to me, but I knew I was supposed to follow them. Once I got inside I was blown away with how beautiful the place was. You saw it and know firsthand that the house was stunning. Anyway, they pointed to the couch. Before I walked towards it they undid the rope around my wrist. I followed the silent order and sat down on the couch. Waiting for what seemed like hours I keep looking around the room; soaking in all the beautiful things. Eventually I was joined by the man you knew as Boss. Surprisingly, he was soft spoken and nice to me. He sat beside me, snapped his fingers, and someone brought us tea and fruit. Of course, I was too afraid to eat or drink anything and I think that upset him a little. He explained why I was there and that he wanted me to feel welcome. I was to do the daily chores and keep the house cleaned. When someone got hurt or needed a nurse I was supposed to attend to them. He told me I would have my own room and could move around the house as I wanted. There were rules of course, so he outlined them. The back door was the only one I could use to go outside, I had to let someone know I was going outside, and I couldn't go past the fence. They would let me outside whenever I wanted and trusted me enough to allow me out there. Last I couldn't enter any rooms upstairs unless directed to do so. That is where they brought all the wounded people in. There were also rules about what foods to give the wounded and what not.

Anyway...

After I was shown my room, given food and water, he sat me down again. He told me that he couldn't trust me just yet and that he would have someone with me at all times until I proved that I was trustworthy. The first night I tried to escape and was caught. No punishment came that time, but the next time wasn't the same.

I tried to climb out of my window that night but got caught by a guard. The guard took me outside and waited for Boss. Once he was outside with me the guard left. He told me that I would be punished that time and any other time after, if I tried to escape. That night it was winter time and snow was beginning to fall. The guards made me take all my clothes off and stand naked in the cold. The worst part was being sprayed with water for what felt like hours. Each time I tried to escape was more awful than the last. Eventually I stopped trying to escape. That was when he felt he could finally trust me, and life on the land became bearable.

I spent the next years working for him and being close to him. He was my only contact and the only person who cared about me at the time. We would talk for hours sometimes about things going on in the world. For me time stopped. I never knew what was going on other than what I saw each day. I don't expect you to understand, but he became a friend to me. When you spend four years with someone day and night you become close to them. Not every experience was good, but it wasn't supposed to be. It never mattered how bad or good he treated me. I was devoted to him and he knew it. Please understand that I am glad he is gone and I'm free, but he wasn't as much of a monster as you think."

With that the conversation ended and I didn't know what to say to her. It was hard for me to understand what she was saying. It was like she was happy to have been there with him all that time. It would be a conversation I would have to have with a therapist and she would have to do the same.

CHAPTER EIGHTEEN

After we ate we headed back to my house. Once again, our car ride was quiet. I kept my eyes on the road, but I kept a close watch on my mother out of the corner of my eye. She hadn't made any indication that she wanted to go see my father, but I knew I had to figure out when and how to tell him the news about her being home. Especially before the news caught on and the word would be out about everything.

"Mama what do you want me to do about Dad?"

Using my free hand, I pushed my hair behind my ears and waited for her to respond. It took a while for her to speak, but she finally responded.

"Blair... I do want to go see him, but I'm just

not sure now is the right time. Maybe I can call him and talk to him, but I'm still not even sure about that."

I understood. He was and always would be the reason she was taken. At least that's the way I saw it in my eyes.

"It's okay Mama. You don't have to worry about that now. I will drop you off at my house and run over to Dad's to explain things to him."

The only response that came was a nod. I took it for what it was worth and didn't speak to my mother again until I got home later that night. My father took the news hard and cried for a while. It took a while to explain everything to him, but I kept as much detail out that I could. It was hard for him to think about what she had been through. It was especially hard for him to accept that she didn't want to see him just yet. Of course, before I left I promised him that I would bring my mother over once she was ready. I was still angry with him, but it was also hard to see the pain he was going through.

Once I got home I found my mother lying on the couch asleep. She was tired, and so was I. It was our first night back, so I wanted to finally sleep in my own bed. My mind kept running wild, because the thought of cameras in my home still haunted me. It was a creepy feeling that I knew would take a while to go away. Once in my room I grabbed my mother a blanket and pillow. Without waking her I covered her up and laid a pillow next to her. With my eyes heavy I started to walk back to my room. A soft knock at the front door stopped me in my tracks.

My heart picked up speed and a scared feeling ran over my body. *Who the hell would be at my house this late at night?* As I walked to the door I could feel my hands ball up into fist and my mind go into fight mode. It was a new habit that would take time to snap out of. I looked through the peep hole and rolled my eyes at who was there. As quiet as I could I opened the door and stepped outside.

There on my door step stood Alex.

"What the fuck do you want?"

"Oh my god Blair what happened to you? I heard about it on the news and came right over."

It felt like steam was coming out of my ears because I was so mad.

"You want to know what happened to me? I got dumped by a cheating boyfriend who slept with my best friend. Then a crazy ass man kidnapped me, and I had to fend for my life. I was hunted like an animal and had to fight to the death. Not only that but I had to save my mother's life and sixty-three others. You and that slimy thing of a man are the reason I was there in the first place; fucking backstabbers. Then you thought it would be a great idea to come by and check on me. Are you that stupid? I don't give two shits about you. I don't want to hear one word from you or him. Now get the fuck off my steps before I make you, and trust me after all the shit I have been through it will be as easy as blinking to handle you."

Alex gave me a shocked look as tears ran down her face. Never saying a word, she turned around and headed to her car.

I went back inside the house and slammed the door. Angry couldn't describe how I felt in that moment. Anger and rage had become normal for me to feel and I had to get it under control. With everything that happened to me, I was finding it hard to adjust back to my normal life. Taking a deep breath, I sat down on the couch trying not to wake my mother. Just as I got my anger under control another knock came at the door. My eyes shot open and I stood up. *Why the hell is she back? Did she not understand the meaning of go away?* I knew I had to be careful or I would lose it on Alex.

I pulled the door back open in a jerking motion. My "go to hell" look was in place, but quickly disappeared. It wasn't Alex at the door like I thought; it was Adam, the man that helped save my life along with so many others. It was almost hard to recognize him, but one look into his eyes and I knew who he was. No more mud was on his body, the blood was washed away, his naked body was covered with clothes, and the scared look in his eyes was replaced with calm. Words weren't able to come to me and I felt my body start to shake. There wasn't any way I could speak and I didn't even know if I could move. He was just as speechless as I was and for a second I wondered if either of us would be able to talk. So many questions came to my mind, but none came out.

In a soft whisper he only said one word, "Blair."

Goose bumps ran over my skin. A smile left my mouth. I moved towards him and wrapped both my arms around him. As I hugged him tight, tears fell from my eyes.

Adam and I shared a bond that no one in the world would ever understand. We had been through hell and had each other in the end. It wasn't a figure of speech whenever I described him by saying, "Without him I would be dead and without me so would he." Pulling away from him I looked into his eyes.

"Adam, what are you doing here?"

He smiled from ear to ear. It was the first time I ever seen him smile and I felt like there was a-whole-nother person standing in front of me.

"I had to find you. I had to say thank you, because I didn't have that chance before. I...I just wanted to see you Blair."

Wiping away the tears I smiled back at him.

"Well don't stand outside, come on in!"

Adam and I spent the rest of the night talking. We didn't talk about anything we had been through. We only spoke about our life before and the life we were going to create with our second chance. For the first time in a while I felt alive talking to him. Time stood still in a good way for once and all the pain we had been through couldn't take away the memories we promised to make in the future. I wasn't sure what would ever bloom from our relationship but I was willing to let it flow in whatever direction it went. Nothing mattered except that we were alive and we had each other.

CHAPTER NINETEEN

Over the next few weeks my mother and I tried to get on with our lives. We saw a therapist twice a week and I went back to work for a few hours a day. My mother stayed at my home and tried to stay busy in everyday things. It hurt me that she wasn't ready for the world yet. I totally understood though, because I didn't want to get out into the world either. Yes, I went to the shelter to check on the animals for a few hours, but that was all I could handle.

It was one of our therapy days and I wasn't looking forward to it. My mother and I were going to be given an evaluation on our progress. Like normal I went home and picked my mother up to go to our appointment. She was quiet. Not wanting to upset her I stayed quiet the whole ride with her.

Once we got there we split ways and went to our own therapist. My therapist, Doctor Wong, was a beautiful Asian lady in her late forties. Her dark long hair was always down and kept away from her face. She always had on nice clothes under her white coat and her voice was always calm, soft, and welcoming. That helped when I spoke to her about what I had been through.

Sitting on the couch I watched her bring a notebook and pen over to her normal chair.

"Blair, let's talk about your mother. We need to address what steps I suggest you take to help integrate her back into society."

I could only nod and wait for answers.

"Your mother is having a tough time at life right now and things are proving to be a challenge for her. She was kept away for four long years by a man she never knew. Doctor Alexander and I both agree on our diagnosis. First let me say that you are improving already, and I think you will recover from this much faster than your mother. Mia, on the other hand, has what we call Stockholm syndrome. Do you know what that is?"

I nodded my head yes, but because of my

confused look, Doctor Wong continued.

"It's where someone develops a love for someone that has hurt them."

Her tone made it sound more of a question than a statement.

"This may be hard for you to hear and possibly understand, but it is necessary for you to know to help her along her road to recovery. In the four years that your mother was there she developed a bond with Rich. He took care of her, mentally and psychically. Yes, he also abused her but that's where this all falls into play. Even through the abuse, she found a connection and developed emotional ties with him. Your mother knows what he did to her is wrong and that's one great first step. Now is the process for her to understand that it's not her fault and that he was the bad guy. For so long she was made to be under his control and now that the control is gone, she has to figure out how to live without him and that's very hard. Things like eating at a certain time, being able to shower more than one time a day, walk outside without a fence around her, and so on are all hard for her to take in. She had to obey him to live each day and he'd implanted into her brain that she would not survive if she tried to escape. There are many methods we can take to help get her back to a normal life Blair, but she can't do it without you."

At that moment I realized that tears had ran down my face while she was talking. I wiped them away and looked into Doctor Wong's eyes.

"Tell me what to do. I just got her back and I won't lose her again."

Doctor Wong nodded and came over to the couch I was sitting on.

"First, she needs to keep seeing Doctor Alexander. It's important that we continue to treat her and help her. Talking about it to a doctor can make a difference. We are not biased, and we don't judge her. I know you wouldn't mean to, but more than likely you would because your experience was different, and your feelings don't match hers. Next, we have to let her know that she doesn't have to be in survival mode all the time. She is free, and we need her to understand that. Try to encourage her to take small steps. Go outside one day and just sit on the grass, let her eat at a time that doesn't match her eating schedule, and try to let her do things on her own. I am here to help you along the way as well."

Doctor Wong paused, placed her hand on my shoulder, and said, "Blair, she will get better, but it will take time. You both went through some terrible things. Thankfully you have each other. You are a survivor and a hero, remember that."

Hero was a strong word in my book but at that moment I could care less what they called me. It was my mother that I worried about the most.

"Okay. You are right I don't understand it, but I love her and am willing to do whatever it takes to help her. Time is something I didn't think I would have again and now I have plenty of it. We are alive and that's all that matters, everything else is just words on a paper."

EPILOGUE

Mia

It was three months later and Mia was finally getting used to Florida. It was a long road, but she was at least trying at life. Mia faithfully saw her psychiatrist every week. She sat in the office waiting for Doctor Alexander to enter. Her feelings were always up and down since she got back home. Life felt complex and she constantly felt like a burden to everyone around her. The only constant in her life was Blair. Mia still lived with her. They enjoyed each other's company and she was more help to Mia than she could ever know.

During Mia's meeting with her doctor and Blair's doctor, they told her to stick to the routine she was used to, but incorporating something new each day. Up until that point it was helping Mia cope with everything a little better. Spending four years of her life like a prisoner was hard but what made it worse was she didn't feel like a prisoner. At first, she did but later she felt safe, calm, and needed like never before. Rich was complicated in so many ways. He was firm with her on the rules, but as long as she followed them he was sweet to her. The doctors had all told her it would take time to understand that what he did to her was wrong.

Time was the only hope she had left to be normal again. Since leaving the hunting land time seemed to move at a snail's pace to Mia. This was especially true when she finally spoke to her husband James. It took almost a month before Mia got up the courage to even go see James. Nevertheless, the meeting was awkward. Not much was said between the two of them due to her being withdrawn and James being emotional. Mia knew it broke something inside of James finding out what she had been through, but seeing him cry was too much for her. There was no way she could be around him; he blamed himself and part of her did as well. After all, it was his cheating that made her leave home that night. Of course, she knew deep down that Rich would have taken her no matter what, but the timing of the affair and her kidnapping only gave her more time to be angry with him over the years.

Doctor Alexander called Mia's name and snapped her back to her reality, away from her thoughts. Mia sighed, stood up, and walked towards the door. She let out a soft smile as she confidentially greeted Doctor Alexander. She was ready to leave her past in the past and ready for her future.

Adam

After everything that happened, Adam went back home and attempted to live a normal life. It was hard because the friends that he did have prior to his abduction insensitively asked him a million questions about what happened to him and he eventually shied away from them. All of his family lived away from him so he was alone. Being alone was not what he wanted and Blair was the only person he could think of that would understand.

Adam moved into town not far from where Blair lived because he wanted a chance to start new. It made sense to them to be close to each other so they could always be there for one another if need be. At first he worried Blair wouldn't want him around because of the painful memories he brought with him, but once they reunited she was happy to see him.

Adam had jumped from job to job during the past three months. It had been hard for him to adjust, so Blair offered him a job at the shelter. Adam walked into the shelter, happy to start his day off there. It was the only job since being free that he didn't feel trapped in. Every other job felt like it was weighing him down and he couldn't cope with it. His therapist said it was to be expected for him to feel that way after going through such a traumatic experience, and eventually a job would stick. Luckily for him, working for Blair stuck with him. He didn't know for sure if it was the animals or Blair but he did not mind either way. The peace of mind was a blessing within itself.

Things over the months had grown between Blair and Adam. They had become each other's therapist. Some days they didn't even bring up any of the bad memories and others they struggled together. Adam felt like moving near Blair was the best decision he ever made. Talking to Blair made things easier to deal with. He owed her his life and he planned to always be there for her; no matter what. He planned to continue his second chance at life moving in the right direction.

Blair

After everything, Blair felt as if something was lacking. There wasn't an easy way to describe it, but she felt like a part of her was left on the hunting land. When she went to the hunting grounds she was a calm, sassy, smart, and fun person. When she came home she was rough around the edges, jumpy, and always on alert. Some days she felt almost normal but everyone had their bad days. Bad days normally ended with her curled up in a corner having flashbacks from her memories. The doctors diagnosed it as post-traumatic stress disorder. They weren't sure it would ever go away, but Blair didn't think it would anytime in the near future.

Luck wasn't a word Blair used lightly after everything that happened, but that word seemed to travel everywhere she, Adam, and Mia went. Blair was determined to push forward. Not only for herself, but for her mother and Adam; they needed her. She knew she would make it with her strength and determination. With a second chance at life she planned to spend it in the right direction. One step at a time she would conquer anything thrown at her.

She did not let Rich win when he was alive and vowed to not along him to win in death.

About The Author
Brianna Johnson

Brianna Johnson is a fresh new up and coming author from a small town in the Virginia Mountains, who now resides in Fountain Inn South Carolina. Brianna always had a passion for books and one day decided to turn that passion in a different direction by writing her debut novel Framed. As a new writer she plans to write many more books in genres including erotica, mystery, romance, and suspense. To learn more about Brianna Johnson visit her Facebook page @Authorbriannajohnson.

Check out these books by Author Brianna Johnson:

FRAMED

FRAMED 2

ALL BOOKS AVAILABLE AT

https://www.amazon.com/Brianna-Johnson/e/B074SC151D

92759219R00105

Made in the USA
Lexington, KY
09 July 2018